# Room for Love

### FOR

# Frankie J.
# JONES

# Room for Love

♦

## Frankie J.
## JONES

## Bella
## BOOKS

Ferndale, Michigan
2001

**Bella Books, Inc.**
P.O. Box 201007
Ferndale, MI 48220

Printed in the United States of America on acid-free paper
First Edition

Editor: Lila Empson
Cover designer: Bonnie Liss (Phoenix Graphics)


ISBN 0-9677753-9-6

## Acknowledgments

Thanks to Rita Granberry for providing me with more information than I ever wanted on birthing babies. Thanks to Peggy J. Herring for being my first reader and to Martha Cabrera for being my second reader and for her support and encouragement during revisions.

# CHAPTER ONE

Jo wiped the sweat from her face with a large red bandanna and appraised the sprawling ranch house with the trained eye of a carpenter. Structurally, it looked sound, but a fresh coat of paint would do wonders for its appearance.

She stepped into the shade of one of the seven ancient oak trees that provided a cool reprieve from the heat and humidity. It was only a little after two, but the temperature had already climbed into the upper nineties. She eyed her battered Ford truck with misgivings — the air conditioner was going to have to be repaired. The South Texas July weather was too hot, and August would be hell.

The faint scent of roses drifted to her from the bushes that

1

bordered the front of the house. Despite the grueling heat and drought, the plants looked lush and well tended.

Jo thought about the rose garden she and Diane had planned. Diane had actually started the planning after listening to Jo's fond memories of her grandmother's roses. She surprised Jo with the plans for a small rose garden that would be just outside the master bedroom of their dream house. French doors would open onto a small patio with a water fountain in the center. The roses would grace three sides of the patio. She and Diane had spent countless hours walking through nurseries and poring over plant catalogs searching for the most fragrant varieties.

Sounds of laughter came from the far side of the house where two men were unloading sacks of grain from a pickup into a large, beige metal shed with a connecting corral running its length. A horse standing in the thin strip of shade drew her attention. She shuddered slightly. Even from this distance the horse looked huge.

Jo had learned from her best friend, Elsie Brown, that Beth Harman, the owner, was divorced and worked the three-hundred-acre ranch with only a foreman and two hired hands.

A movement beside the house caught Jo's attention. A young girl dressed in a pink-and-white striped sleeveless top and pink shorts walked slowly toward her. Jo guessed her to be five or six years old. The child stopped several feet from Jo and threw a hesitant glance back at the house before looking again at the woman before her. Jo realized the child was probably debating whether she should talk to her or call someone from the house.

"Hello," Jo called, hoping to ease the child's anxiety.

"Hi." The girl shaded her large, brown eyes with a grubby hand to stare up at Jo's tall, solid frame.

"Is your mom home? I'm Jo Merrick. I'm here to see her about doing some work."

"I'm Tracy," the child answered with a bright smile.

2

"Mom's in the house talkin' to Ernie. Come on." She took Jo's hand and started walking. "Mom thinks you're a man," Tracy said with a giggle.

"Well, a lot of people get confused by my name. I guess Elsie forgot to mention it."

Elsie Brown owned a real estate agency in San Antonio and had heard through her vast network of contacts that Mrs. Harman was looking for someone to build an additional room onto her place. With some misgivings, Jo had agreed to drive the eighty miles between San Antonio and the ranch near Dodson to talk to Mrs. Harman about the job. Work was slow, and she needed to stay busy. The money would help in the added expense of repairing her truck's air conditioner, but money was secondary to Jo. Her small house was paid for, and her expenses were few. Her lifestyle was simple, and she liked it that way. Her pressing need was simply to work. To keep herself so busy there wasn't time for memories of Diane's death to invade.

In the process of becoming a workaholic, Jo also became a loner. Elsie was the only person she had allowed to enter her life, and she held even Elsie at a safe distance.

"Whatcha gonna do for my Mom?" Tracy asked, interrupting Jo's thoughts.

"I'm not sure, but I think she wants to add on a room." Jo studied the large house. "Looks like you have plenty of space already."

"Oh, it's on the cabin."

"The cabin?"

"Uh-huh. Mom wants to make it bigger so I can have my very own room. I'm too old to share a room now." With a new sense of importance, Tracy pulled the screen door open and stopped. "You stay here. I'm not supposed to let strangers in, so I'll go get her. She's sure gonna be surprised you ain't, uh, you're not a man."

The child looked around guiltily. "Mom says I'm not

3

supposed to say *ain't* no more. I get a dollar if I can go a whole week without sayin' it." She looked down at her tanned bare feet. "Guess I already lost my dollar," she said with a sad sigh.

Jo knelt down and took one of Tracy's small hands. "I think you remembered to correct it in time. Mistakes are only bad if you don't bother to fix them. So you're okay."

Tracy looked up and flashed her a bright smile. "Yeah!" She shot inside, leaving Jo smiling after her.

Jo experienced a moment of anxiety wondering if her being a woman would matter to Mrs. Harman. Construction was still a man's world, and some people thought gender was a direct reflection on ability.

She leaned against the peeling porch rail to wait for Beth Harman and began to construct a mental list of where she would look for work if this job fell through.

The house was up on a slight hill that allowed a wonderful view of the surrounding countryside. The landscape was beautiful even though it was dry and baked from the lack of rain. Diane would have liked the view, Jo thought. Diane had been able to find a spark of beauty in the barest of landscapes. Jo took a deep breath and let it out slowly. It had been a year and eleven months since Diane's death.

A cool breeze ruffled Jo's short, auburn hair as she corralled the thoughts of Diane and gently placed them behind one of the mental walls she had built to protect herself.

At the sound of the screen door opening, Jo turned to find a slender woman who was almost as tall as Jo's own five-feet-nine-inch frame. Her waist-length brown hair was pulled back and held in a single braid. She looked completely at ease in worn jeans, a plaid cotton shirt, a battered hat, and scruffy work boots. This was a woman who didn't need external trappings to feel secure.

"Yes?" she said, staring at Jo with the same intense, dark brown eyes as her child's.

4

"I'm Jo Merrick." Jo saw the name didn't register. "The carpenter."

"Oh. I'm sorry. I was expecting, uh ..." Beth's surprise was evident, but Jo gave her credit for trying to cover it.

"A man." Jo supplied the missing word.

Beth blushed a deep crimson before extending her hand. "Forgive me. I shouldn't have assumed. Walter failed to mention you were a woman."

Jo assumed Walter must be Elsie's contact. "Elsie probably never told him," she said.

"Come inside out of the heat."

Jo realized she was still holding Beth's hand and quickly released it. As they stepped into the house, Jo saw Tracy standing just inside the doorway and gave her a quick wink, causing the child to giggle.

"Where are your shoes?" Beth asked, spying Tracy's bare feet.

Tracy eyed her feet as she dug her toes into the thick blue carpet. "My feet got hot."

"Go play," Beth conceded with a sigh, mussing Tracy's short, curly hair before leading Jo into a large study.

A man stood bent over a table, deeply engrossed in a thick set of ledgers. The room was decorated in soft earth tones. Rag rugs provided brilliant splashes of color in front of the couch and a recliner. Sand paintings decorated the light oak paneling.

Diane hated paneling. She would have ripped it out. Jo shook her head to brush away her thoughts. She noticed how cool the house was with only the windows and doors opened. The design of the house allowed it to catch even the slightest breeze. Why can't my truck be this cool? she wondered in exasperation.

"This is my foreman, Ernie Stanton." Beth introduced a short, thin man Jo guessed to be in his late fifties. He looked up from the ledgers he was studying. His wrinkled, leathery face testified to the countless hours he had spent in the sun. "This is the carpenter, Jo Merrick."

"Hello," Ernie said in a quiet voice as he shook Jo's hand. His sky-blue eyes hinted at a boyish mischief.

Going to a corner Beth picked up a roll of blueprints. She spread them out on a long, wooden table that sat behind the couch.

"I want to add a room onto the cabin. Here's what I need." Ernie and Jo moved to either side of her.

The smell of roses engulfed Jo. It took a moment for Jo to realize that it was the woman beside her and not the plants outside. A sense of loneliness invaded her, and she found herself leaning into the scent. Embarrassed, she pulled up sharply.

Damn, she thought. At this rate I'll be climbing into her lap and asking for a peppermint.


Jo's maternal grandmother had always smelled of roses and peppermint. The smell of roses came from the small, tightly tied bundles Jo would find when she peeked into dresser drawers filled with delicate lace and silk shawls.

Jo remembered crawling into her grandmother's lap and burying her face in her shoulder, surrounded by the smell of roses and peppermint. Her grandmother would laugh and stroke Jo's hair with one hand while digging with the other into her apron pocket for a piece of the sweet, pungent peppermint.

Jo sucked on the candy while her grandmother told her the importance of hard work and determination, stressing how those two factors had allowed her to escape the harsh poverty of Ireland and come to America where she met and

6

married Jo's grandfather. Together they worked hard to raise two equally hard-working and determined sons. After reinforcing those traits her grandmother would tell Jo about the old country. While safely tucked against her grandmother's warm body, Jo would become lost in a magical world of wily leprechauns, enchanted forests, and bright pots of gold.

Confused by her inability to control her emotions, Jo refocused her attention on the blueprints with single-minded determination. She needed to erase everything but the thought of work from her mind.

"It's nothing fancy," Beth was continuing. "I want to make this window a doorway that leads into the new room. The room will be ten-by-ten, and I want a large closet for storage right here." She tapped the blueprints to indicate where she wanted the closet and stepped back to let Jo examine the plans. What Beth hadn't told Jo, the blueprints did. The room was a simple square design, with one window and a closet, nothing elaborate or difficult.

Beth waited silently until Jo completed her study.

"I'd like to see the cabin before I decide whether to submit an estimate," Jo said, letting the blueprints roll back up. She needed to examine the condition of the structure before agreeing to take the job and offering a price. She didn't want to commit herself to a project that would be better suited to demolition. Termites and the South Texas weather had undermined the structural integrity of buildings to the point of their near collapse. And if this was just some hunter's cabin that was used once or twice a year, it probably wasn't in very good shape.

"We could ride out now if you have time," Beth said, glancing at her watch.

"Sure."

Beth turned to Ernie. "Would you ask Carl to bring up two horses for us?"

"Horses!" Jo shrieked louder than she had intended and felt herself blushing at Ernie's amused smile.

"The cabin is up in the hills, and it's not accessible from here by car. It's either horseback or walking. You can ride, can't you?" A slight, teasing smile played across Beth's lips.

The question and Beth's attitude pricked Jo's pride. "Of course, I can ride." She wouldn't admit that she was afraid of horses. Or that putting herself at the mercy of an animal weighing several hundred pounds with a mind of its own wasn't logical. Jo's limited experience with horses had shown her that they do exactly as they please, including throwing her butt in the dirt at any given moment and taking off without a backward glance.

Which was exactly what had happened during her only attempt at riding twelve years ago. The mere size of the animal had intimidated Jo from the beginning. Having grown up in the city she had no experience with animals except for the odd hamster, cat, or dog.

After a reluctant start from the stable, the horse had stopped to munch on every clump of grass they happened upon. With the horse's continuous grazing she had quickly fallen behind the woman she had gone riding with. The woman was the reason Jo was attempting to ride a horse in the first place. Jo had been trying to impress her. The entire day had been a disaster. She cringed when she remembered that her experience with the horse had actually turned out a lot better than it had with the woman.

\* \* \* \* \*

Jo wasn't about to climb back up on one of those beasts for anyone. She turned to Beth.

"How do you plan on getting lumber and supplies in if it's so remote? Plus, I'll need electricity for my tools," Jo informed her.

"There's a road that goes in on the far side of the property, and the cabin has electricity. Dad had it installed years ago."

"Great. Give me directions. I'll drive around and meet you there," Jo said.

Beth slid her hands into her hip pockets. "It's a sixty-mile drive to get to the other side from here. We'd have to go all the way to Dodson and around. The last twenty miles or so is a dirt road that's next to impassable. If we go overland on horseback it's less than an hour."

Jo had the feeling that Beth was using the same patient tone of voice she'd use if explaining something to Tracy, and it irritated her. Why should she have to feel defensive about not wanting to ride a horse?

"As for lumber and supplies," Beth continued, oblivious to Jo's irritation. "Almost everything you need has been brought in already and the foundation has been poured. All that remains is to get a carpenter up there."

A slight falter in her voice told Jo there had been no other estimates offered. No one else wanted to ride a horse to work either, she thought with a childish sense of satisfaction.

"I don't want to have to ride to work on horseback for an hour every day." Jo tried not to snap, but she wanted — no needed — a physically demanding job like this to keep her busy through the second anniversary of Diane's death. She could lose herself in the work during the day, and the physical exhaustion brought on by working hard would allow her to sleep at night. A perfect job for her.

Besides that, she knew she could build the room cheaper than most large contractors since she didn't have the overhead they had to contend with and she would do a better job in workmanship.

She had planned on talking to a friend about using his nearby hunting cabin while working here. That would have solved the problem of the long daily commute to and from San Antonio. And now, because of this stubborn woman and her silly horses, Jo would have to drive back in the stifling heat and start looking for another job.

"Why would you want a cabin that remote?" She knew it was none of her business, but she was disgusted at having wasted the entire day and she still faced the long, hot drive home.

"Because I like privacy." Beth's hands slid from her pockets, only to be planted squarely on her hips. Her own irritation was growing more obvious.

Jo had a brief thought that here was a woman who was used to getting her own way and didn't like to have her decisions questioned.

"You won't be riding in and out every day," Beth continued. "*If* you get the job, *we* will be staying at the cabin."

Jo didn't miss the emphasis on *if* and *we*, but Beth cut off her thoughts before she could comment.

"If you can't handle the job, Ms. Merrick, I'll find another carpenter."

Shocked by Beth's suggestion that she was hesitating because she couldn't handle the job rankled Jo further. "I'm quite capable of handling the job, Mrs. Harman. I'm just not sure I want it." They stood glaring at each other while Jo mentally berated herself. Of course you want the job, you idiot. You're just too damn stubborn and scared to ride the horse.

"Then why don't you go see?" Ernie's calm voice cut in. Both women turned to stare at him. He had been so quiet that Jo had forgotten he was in the room.

Jo and Beth glanced at each other before quickly looking away. Jo was embarrassed. Why had she gotten so upset? She

10

wanted this job. With the slump in construction, it wouldn't be easy to find a job that would carry her through the next few weeks. It's the heat, she told herself. It's making me irritable. That and the pending anniversary of Diane's death.

"It's up to you," Beth said, her voice once more calm. "We could drive all the way around to Dodson, but it'll be dark before we can get back. Maybe we should plan on going another day." She dug the toe of her boot into the carpet as Tracy had done with her toes earlier.

The simple act affected Jo in much the same way as it had Beth when Tracy did it. Jo felt her animosity melt away. It was ridiculous to let something as simple as riding a horse keep her from working. She didn't want to drive back up here at a later date. Riding the horse to the cabin would be a one-time thing and besides, she reminded herself, she wanted this job.

"I guess we could ride over and look at it today," Jo said. She sounded brave enough, but her stomach still dropped freestyle at the thought of getting near a horse.

Ernie nodded and turned to leave. "I'll get the horses."


Jo watched Beth swing into the saddle with an easy grace that told of her confidence in a saddle. With more than a little trepidation, Jo approached the gray mare Ernie held for her. She took a deep breath and tried to shake off her nervousness when Ernie extended the reins to her.

"This is Blossom," he said, patting the mare's neck. He leaned closer and whispered, "She's as gentle as a newborn baby. She won't go anywhere you don't tell her to."

"Could I have that in writing?" Jo asked, her voice dripping with skepticism. Ernie chuckled as Jo placed her foot in the stirrup and pulled herself up with much less finesse than Beth had.

Tracy came running up clutching an old, battered Stetson.

"I brought this for you to wear," she explained, handing the hat up to Jo.

"Thank you," Jo said and plopped the hat on her head. She had never liked hats and would have preferred not to use it, but Tracy looked so proud that Jo she couldn't refuse.

"You got it on backwards," Tracy said with a giggle.

"Oh." Knowing she was probably smirking at her ignorance, Jo refused to look at Beth Harman. Her face grew red as she fumbled to turn the hat around.

"Can I go?" Tracy asked Beth.

"Have you finished cleaning your room?"

Tracy rolled her eyes and started walking back toward the house. "I don't know why I have to clean it. It's just gonna get dirty again."

With a wave to Ernie, Beth headed out across a wide, sun-parched pasture.

Jo gave Ernie one last pleading glance. He shook his head and laughed before giving Blossom a light slap on the rump. Jo clung to the reins and saddle horn as the mare broke into a gentle trot behind Beth.


They rode in silence. Jo eventually relaxed enough to tear her eyes from the ground before her and glanced at the hot, glaring sky. She wished it would rain. It hadn't rained in San Antonio in over a month and the vegetation didn't look as if it had rained here either.

As the time slipped by and the mare maintained a slow, steady gait behind Beth, Jo began to relax and enjoy the ride. She loved this area with its steep hills and wide valleys. She and Diane had once talked of buying land by a nearby lake.

The familiar emptiness swept over her. Will it ever stop hurting? she wondered. She blinked tears away and focused her attention on the faint trail they were following. As the terrain grew rockier and steeper, the insides of her legs started to hurt. She tried to shift and relax her leg muscles, but the trail grew steeper and they ached more. She wished Beth would stop for a rest. Her own stubborn pride kept her from requesting that they do so. She had already whined enough for one day. Jo pulled her hat down farther over her eyes to block the sun's glare. She would have to remember to thank Tracy again for loaning it to her. She would have really been miserable without it.

Several minutes later, Beth finally drew her horse to a halt and climbed down. They were on a wide slope that was covered in dark green junipers and ancient oaks.

"Let's rest the horses for a while."

Grateful beyond words, Jo slipped to the ground. Her legs trembled, so she had to hold onto the saddle for support. There goes my theory about being in great shape, she chided herself. She had assumed that years of lifting and swinging lumber and heavy bags of cement mix had prepared her for anything, but it hadn't prepared her for this.

"Are you all right?" Beth called.

"I'm great," she chirped. "Just goddamn great," she added in a mumble. Praying her wobbly legs would support her, Jo released her grip on the saddle and began to walk in small circles trying to ease the pain.

"There's fresh water in your canteen."

"Thanks." Jo pulled down the canvas-covered canteen. The water was cold. She closed her eyes and savored the sensation of the water's cool journey across her tongue and down her throat. She imagined herself as a large human sponge soaking up the liquid. As the coolness sank to her stomach Jo opened her eyes.

She saw Beth pour water into her beat-up hat and hold it for her horse to drink. Jo hesitated and then mimicked her actions. The mare drank noisily and nudged her nose against the empty hat when she had consumed the small amount of water Jo had given her. Jo grunted and poured more water into the hat.

"Guess I shouldn't be so stingy since you're the one who's been doing all the work," she said, holding the hat in one hand and tentatively reaching out with her other to rub the animal's neck. The shiny coat rippled beneath her touch. Encouraged that the horse hadn't attacked her, Jo scratched the area behind Blossom's ear. Blossom rewarded her with a soft snort of contentment.

When the horse had finished drinking, Jo shook out the hat and placed it on the saddle horn. Her legs were trembling less, so she began to walk about. Beth stretched out on the grass beneath an oak tree and closed her eyes. She looked so comfortable that Jo decided to join her.

The air was a little cooler up here in the higher altitude than it had been at the ranch, and the grass still held a touch of green. It felt good on the backs of Jo's arms. She shifted her legs and tried to get comfortable. Her jeans were soaked with sweat and were beginning to chafe her legs.

Working outside for long stretches kept her skin deeply tanned, so she didn't worry about sunburn; although now, she was beginning to worry about all the articles she'd been seeing on skin cancer. Memories of the diagnosis, numerous radiation treatments, and Diane's tears of pain assaulted her. Without warning a chill swept over her. She rubbed the goose bumps off her arms and hopped up. "I'm ready when you are."

Beth peeked from under her hat. A small frown creased her forehead. "Sure you don't want to rest a while longer?"

"No. I'm fine." Jo answered, already climbing into the saddle.

Beth shrugged and walked to her horse. Jo watched as Beth tightened the cinch and swung into the saddle.

"The trail gets a little steeper before it levels off," Beth called as she headed out. At the moment Jo didn't care; she just wanted to be moving. She soon changed her mind.

\* \* \* \* \*

14

The trail wound up the hill at a sharp angle, gradually becoming narrower until it tapered to a four-foot ledge. Jo clung to the saddle horn and eyed the sickening drop-off. She estimated the drop to be over two hundred feet. At the bottom she could see a massive pile of rocks that she was certain had once been a part of this ledge. She wondered briefly what caused them to break away. An earthquake maybe? Or had they simply lost the ongoing battle with time and plummeted to the jagged floor below?

She studied the face of the wall beside her and the ledge they were traveling along. A cold sweat trickled down the nape of her neck as she saw the deep fissures in the rocks. One crack in the ledge in front of her caused Jo's heart to skip a couple of beats. Without fully realizing she had done so, she pulled the reins and brought the horse to a halt. Blossom's front hooves were mere inches from the crack.

At the point where the ledge butted up against the wall, the crack was little more than a line in the rock. It ran across the entire width of the four-foot pathway, until it grew to a width of almost two inches at the edge, where it disappeared over the side of the ledge.

As Jo sat staring at the crack, Beth made a clicking sound with her tongue and Blossom started forward. Surprised and frightened by the horse's sudden movement, Jo grabbed the saddle horn. She watched terrified as Blossom's hooves came down over the crack in the ledge. Jo could only watch and wait for the rock to give under the animal's weight and send them plunging to the bottom. Blossom took one step and then another and another. The crack held and they passed safely onward. Jo realized she had been holding her breath; she slowly released it. She could hear her heart pounding. She would have preferred to have gotten down and walked, but she was afraid to attempt it, scared her movements would frighten the animal and get her tossed over the edge.

"Let Blossom have her head. She'll follow me," Beth called back. "There's only a short stretch of this."

Jo rolled her eyes and tried not to stare down at the long drop. She had no choice but to follow; there wasn't room to turn around. She told herself to stop thinking about what would happen if the horse slipped or was frightened by something. As she clung to the saddle, she recalled the feeling of helplessness she had experienced when she had been thrown from a horse years earlier — the sense of flying head-over-heels through space with no control. What would it be like to drop two hundred feet? She squeezed her eyes shut, and her legs instinctively tightened around the horse, causing Blossom's pace to pick up. Jo immediately eased the pressure.

"It keeps getting wider from here," Beth called out.

With her heart in her throat, Jo forced her eyes open and was relieved to find that the trail was indeed beginning to widen. As the trail continued to expand, Jo made herself relax. She loosened her grip on the saddle and let the mare carry her behind Beth.

"There it is," Beth called a few minutes later and pointed down to a small valley.

Emotionally exhausted, Jo reined in beside her and caught her breath. Grudgingly, she admitted to herself that the place was beautiful.

The cabin sat on a small rise in a grove of juniper trees. A wide, green meadow separated it from the river that ran behind it. Even in the middle of summer in the scorching heat the landscape was still green.

"It's worth an hour on horseback, isn't it?" Beth asked without taking her eyes off the valley.

Jo sensed Beth's question didn't require an answer. And certainly not the one that Jo would have been inclined to give, that although the valley was beautiful it certainly wasn't worth the terrifying ride she had just experienced.

They rode down into the valley and tied the horses to a

tree before walking around the cabin. Jo refrained from dropping to her knees and kissing the ground, but the thought did occur to her. As she looked around the place she found herself being caught up in its beauty and serenity.

The concrete foundation shone stark against the green landscape. Jo pulled away a few wooden shakes on the outside cabin wall to examine the lumber beneath. The cabin was crudely built but appeared to be solid.

"The lumber on this wall appears to still be in good shape, so I don't think you'll have to replace any of it. The shakes on this side will have to come off, though." Jo closely examined the new foundation. "Whoever poured this did a good job." She caught a whiff of roses again.

"I hired a guy from Dodson," Beth said, sliding her hands into her pockets.

Jo stepped over to the window to check its framing. It would be easy to convert the window into a doorway that would lead from the main cabin into the new room.

"Listen," Beth called as Jo continued her inspection. "If you're willing to take the job and we can agree on a price, I'd like to get you to do it." She was pushing at the dirt with the toe of her boot. "This will probably sound sexist, but I'd rather hire a woman to do the work. I feel more comfortable working with women."

Jo turned to say something, but whatever she had been about to say was forgotten as she turned and saw Beth. She was standing at Jo's left. Her hands were still in her hip pockets and her head was tilted to one side as if waiting for Jo to answer. She had removed her hat, and the long braid had fallen over her shoulder and was lying along the curve of her left breast. A few stray tendrils of hair were plastered to her forehead. Jo experienced an almost overwhelming desire to reach over and slowly unbraid Beth's hair.

Flustered by her sudden feelings, Jo ran her hand through her own sweat-dampened hair. What was that all about? And

17

where did it come from? she asked herself. She hadn't experienced feelings like those since Diane. She realized Beth was waiting for her answer.

"I'll give you an estimate," she mumbled, before turning her attention back to the window, but not quickly enough to avoid noticing the hint of cleavage that peeked from the top of Beth's shirt as she turned away.

Jo pretended to study the cabin wall as she tried to understand what had just happened. Beth Harman was a beautiful woman. She didn't possess the weak, anorexic look that seemed so popular with today's fashion market, but instead displayed more of a fresh I-know-what-I-want kind of demeanor that Jo had always found attractive.

Elsie had said Beth was divorced. What's that got to do with anything? she wondered, and gave herself a sharp reprimand. To distract her rampant thoughts, she pointed to a tarp spread over a large bulk. "Is that the lumber?"

Beth nodded.

"I'll need to make a list of what you've bought before I can give you an estimate."

"I should have everything you need inside," Beth said. She pulled a key from her pocket and disappeared inside the cabin.

Jo gazed at the river, trying to corral her rampant thoughts, until Beth returned with a thin, green ledger.

"This is a complete list. I think you'll find everything you need is here."

Jo took the ledger and scanned it, determined to ignore the faint pleasing smell of roses that clung to Beth. The list of lumber and supplies looked as though it was close to being complete.

"I'll have to check this against the blueprints," she said, closing the ledger and handing it back to Beth. Jo pulled the tarp away and was met by the fresh clean smell of new lumber. She was transported back to the dream home that she was building and Diane was going to decorate. They had dreamed of building and expanding the house as the business of Merrick Construction grew.

Jo's father had been a master carpenter. He had worked hard to build up his own small construction company. As a child and on into her teen years, Jo had tagged along behind him, watching, helping, and learning. She loved the smell of new lumber and the solid dependable feel of a well-balanced hammer in her hand. She thrived on the hard physical labor involved in lifting and handling the lumber. The whine of saws and power tools was as sweet to her ears as any classical composition. There was an almost sensual feel to a well-sanded floor or a perfectly planed board. The smell of cedar or pine was sweeter than any perfume money could buy.

Jo Merrick loved her profession. When her father, who had specialized in residential contracts, retired he had turned Merrick Construction over to his only child. Jo applied the hard work her grandmother had told her about so many years before and expanded her market to include commercial contracts. They were small buildings at first, but she had eventually started taking on larger contracts. She quickly earned a reputation of being honest and dependable like her father. She gradually added a second crew to her payroll, and within four years she had doubled the size of the business.

Her greatest joy had been starting the construction of the house she and Diane had dreamed of.

But all that was gone. Diane was dead. Their dream house was now a charred foundation, and Merrick Construction was nothing more than a one-person minor carpentry business.

Jo dropped the two-by-four she had unconsciously pressed to her cheek and flung the tarp back over the lumber. Diane's ghost didn't usually invade her thoughts so often anymore. She suspected the pending anniversary was causing the increase in flashbacks.

"What do you think?" Beth asked, startling Jo out of her reverie.

"The lumber is fine. Good cut, well seasoned . . ."

"The job," Beth interrupted. She tossed the braid over her shoulder. "Will you do it?"

"You haven't heard my estimate yet," Jo said, arching her eyebrows at Beth's impatience.

"Walter Sanders assured me you came highly recommended. That you were both a fantastic carpenter and honest."

"I'll have to thank Elsie for the excellent PR," Jo said. "But, there's still the matter of hiring an assistant. I'll need help raising the walls and with the roof."

"You won't need to hire anyone. I'll be here to help you," Beth stated.

Jo blinked in surprise and realized that Beth had actually alluded to working alongside Jo earlier. "Mrs. Harman, construction may look simple, but it's hard work. I'm going to need someone who knows at least a little bit about what they're doing."

Beth's hands slipped back into her hip pockets. Jo was beginning to recognize this as a sign that Beth was growing impatient.

"I've worked on this ranch all my life. It's true I have Ernie and two hired hands to help me, but there's not a single job here that I can't and haven't done. As for my construction experience, I helped my father build this cabin. And as you can see he wasn't very skilled in construction. I can see no reason why you need to hire someone else. Plus, if I'm on-site I'll be available if any questions should come up or modifications need to be made."

Jo exhaled sharply. This woman was unbelievable. She had to have everything her way. Jo's first impulse was to tell her where to stick her cabin, but she gritted her teeth. After all, there was no reason for them *both* to act like five-year-olds.

"I'll call you with an estimate tomorrow," Jo said. In spite of everything, she found herself liking Beth Harman's spunk.

# CHAPTER TWO

Later that night, Jo sat soaking in a tub of hot water trying to ease the pain in her legs and butt. She had worked up an estimate and would call Beth Harman tomorrow morning. If the bid was accepted, she wouldn't turn down the work; a perverse part of her, however, hoped Beth would say it was too high. This woman had made her angry, and that scared her.

Jo had kept her emotions in a tight cocoon for over two years, and no one had been able to penetrate it — until Beth Harman. Jo wasn't ready to crawl out of her emotional hibernation just yet. She needed to maintain the emotionally sterile existence she had created for herself. To feel was to hurt. Her struggle to block the pain had been a long, hard battle that she wasn't ready to give up.

Tracy was a cute kid, and it would be easy for Jo to let herself become attached to her, but then the job would end and Tracy would be gone. She wouldn't have to be, a tiny voice nagged.

Frustrated, Jo got out of the tub and vigorously toweled herself dry. Knowing sleep was still hours away, she headed into her utilitarian kitchen to make a fresh pot of coffee.

She sat at the table sipping the strong brew and studying the estimate sheet. She had to admit, now that the trip on horseback was over it hadn't been too bad except for that short stretch of narrow ledge. Besides, she would be going through Dodson in her truck from now on. She would need it to haul her tools. So why was she so hesitant to take this job? She sighed and rubbed her face.

The truth was she didn't want to spend that much time alone with Beth. The thought of spending so much time with someone made her uncomfortable. She rarely went anywhere except to work or out looking for work. Of the people she and Diane had known, only Elsie had kept prodding her to get out more until Jo had grown tired of her badgering and given in.

Jo sat back in her chair and spun her pencil on the tabletop. The overhead light reflected a warm yellow glow from the spinning pencil. The glow reminded her of Tracy's bright smile. It would be so easy to like her. Jo had a soft spot for kids, and there had been a time when she had considered the possibility of having a child of her own. Snatching up the pencil, she erased some of the numbers on her original estimate and added an extra thousand dollars for labor.

"There. That should send Beth Harman looking for another carpenter." The decision left her with an odd sense of relief followed by a disturbing feeling of disappointment. She toyed with the pencil. It wasn't ethical to add that much of a profit.

Why should this job be any different from any other one she had done in the last two years? Beth and Tracy Harman would become problems only if she let them. She could prevent any emotional involvement with them.

She changed the numbers back to the original estimate.

With her conscience intact, she wandered into the living room and settled down on the tattered couch to join her nightly companion — a late-night movie. Sleep came much later.

The television woke her the next morning. Unwilling to move her sore muscles, she lay still. The ancient air conditioner had stopped working again during the night, and she was drenched in sweat. She'd have to go bang on the motor.

A twittering of laughter from the television caused her to peer from under her arm. She was met by the pasted-on smile of the morning all-American male newscaster.

"Entirely too early," she groaned. While fumbling for the remote control, she knocked the cold cup of coffee off the couch arm. "Damn it to hell!" She stumbled to the kitchen for a handful of paper towels to blot the mess from the already disreputable carpet. Her aching muscles protested each movement.

Jo had bought this house after Diane had died. She had intended to fix it up, but had never gotten around to doing so. Somehow it didn't seem to matter anymore. Bending over brought a painful reminder of yesterday's excursion. She cursed her stupidity for riding the horse and then, for good measure, cursed the horse and Beth Harman. The newscaster gave another hearty laugh. She cursed him, too.

She spent ten minutes pounding on the air conditioner's motor before it finally kicked in.

Jo glanced around the yard and felt a twinge of guilt. It was in sad shape. Even the weeds were dying from lack of water. She and Diane had spent hours working in the yard of the tiny house they had rented for four years.

23

She considered turning on the sprinkler before realizing she didn't even know where the water hose was. It was probably in storage with her furniture. Jo had not been able to face looking at the furniture she and Diane had shared. Everything had been placed in storage. She was living with a hodgepodge of used furniture she had purchased at garage sales and used furniture stores.

Jo turned her back on the pathetic landscape. Diane would be disappointed with how she was living. She pushed the thought away and went back inside.

Miserable in her damp clothes, she stripped and stood in the shower, letting the cold water beat down on her. She gradually increased the water's temperature until hot water pounded out the stiffness in her muscles.

A little after ten, she dialed Beth Harman's number. Tracy answered.

"Hello, Tracy. This is Jo Merrick. I came by to see your mom yesterday. Is she in?"

"Yeah. She's in the bathroom right now."

"Tracy!" Beth Harman's voice shrieked.

"Oh. She's through now."

Jo stifled her amusement as Beth took the phone.

"Hello. May I help you?"

"Jo Merrick. I'm calling with the estimate."

A slight pause occurred before Beth spoke. "Hi. I hadn't expected to hear from you so soon."

"The estimate was fairly easy to compile since you had the lumber and I didn't have to find an assistant." Jo experienced a brief stab of panic and almost quoted her the inflated figure, but honesty prevailed and she gave the true estimate.

Beth was silent for so long that Jo began to squirm. Maybe Beth had changed her mind and didn't want Jo to do the job. Or maybe the estimate was more that she had anticipated.

"I'd like to start in two weeks," Beth said at last.

Jo experienced a rush of mixed feelings. She was happy to

get the job. She tried to tell herself that she needed it to stay busy, but a small part of her recognized the fact that she looked forward to seeing Beth and Tracy again. However, the two-week delay would leave her at loose ends during the time she dreaded most.

"Two weeks is a long time to wait, Mrs. Harman. That means I won't be able to take on any other jobs except small ones, and those are pretty hard to find."

Once more Beth was silent. Then she said, "The house needs painting, and there may be some minor repairs to be done. If you're willing to do them, there may be enough to keep you busy for two weeks." Without waiting for Jo's response, Beth raced on. "You're welcome to use the guest room. That will save you from having to drive back and forth, and of course I'll pay you extra."

Jo's heart pounded. Live in the same house as Beth and Tracy for two weeks and then another couple of weeks while the room was being built. That doubled the amount of time they would be spending together. Could she be around them that long and not develop emotional attachments to them?

"I'll start Monday morning, if it's all right with you," Jo found herself saying.

"Fine. If I'm not here, Ernie can show you around. I'll pick up the paint today and have it ready for you."


Monday morning Jo got a late start. Beth and Tracy were gone when she arrived, but Ernie hauled out the paint for Jo. She was on a ladder scraping the eaves at the back of the house when Tracy came bounding up.

"Ernie told us you were here," she announced with her ever-present cheer. "We went to town to get me new school clothes, and Mom bought me a new puppy, too." She held up a small brown-and-white stuffed dog for Jo's inspection.

25

Jo crawled down off the ladder and wiped her hands on her shorts before taking the toy and pretending to study it in great detail. "This is quite an animal."

Tracy beamed.

"I'll have to show you how to build her a doghouse."

Tracy's smile faded. "She don't need a house. She's not real, so she can stay in my room. But someday when I get big I'm gonna have my very own real puppy."

"I thought every ranch had five or six dogs and a dozen cats running around."

"We used to have a dog, Buster, but he died and now I can't have another one."

"Why not?"

"Janet's allergic to dogs, and Mom says we can't get one for a while, just in case she comes back."

Jo instinctually knew she probably wasn't supposed to be hearing all of that and changed the subject. "What are you going to name her?"

Tracy's tiny forehead knitted in deep thought. "Shelly," she said finally.

"Shelly. Why Shelly?"

"There's this girl at school who has big ears just like these." She wiggled the animal's ears. "And her name's Shelly."

Jo hid her amusement. "Listen, maybe it's best you don't tell anyone else why you named her Shelly. It'll be our secret."

The child smiled and agreed.

"Where did you get those big, beautiful eyes?" Jo teased, brushing Tracy's hair away from her face.

"Janet said I've got eyes like my mom."

"And Tracy said she would change her clothes when she got home," Beth scolded, stepping behind Tracy and running her hands over the child's hair.

Jo had failed to hear her approach and was surprised by the sudden irregular beat her heart had developed when she took in Beth's crisp white shorts and a pale blue tank top.

White sandals had replaced the scruffy work boots. Jo suddenly felt self-conscience in her sweaty, paint-stained T-shirt and cutoffs.

"We named my puppy Shelly," Tracy announced with pride.

Beth grimaced. "Shelly, huh? Well, go change your clothes and we'll talk about it later."

Tracy skipped off, swinging Shelly by a floppy ear.

"I'm afraid she'll talk your ear off if you let her," Beth said, smiling after the child.

"Nothing wrong with that. I enjoy talking to her," Jo replied, her thoughts on the elusive Janet. Who was she? She looked at Beth wondering. Could she be a lesbian? And what difference would that make? Jo asked herself with an impatient swipe of the bandanna across her face.

"Did you find everything you needed?" Beth asked, pointing to the paint cans and bags of supplies.

"Yeah. That should do." Jo put the bandanna back into her pocket before running a hand through her short hair, trying to dislodge some of the paint chips. She had suddenly found she didn't want to look so disheveled in front of Beth.

"How long do you think it'll take you to finish?" Beth asked, a frown creasing her forehead as she squinted up at the back of the house where Jo had been scraping.

"Five, maybe six days. But I honestly don't think you have enough work to keep me busy for two weeks."

Beth pinched her lower lip, deep in thought. "If I leave Ernie in charge of handling the shipment of cattle I'm selling, Tracy and I could leave for the cabin late Sunday afternoon. It'll be closer for you to drive straight to the cabin from San Antonio rather than coming here and then going around. We could start Monday. Unless you have something you need to take care of first," she hastened to add.

"No. That's fine with me. I'll need to have my truck to haul in my tools anyway." Jo found herself watching the hollow of Beth's throat. It was a shade darker than the soft part just above it. She tore her eyes away and forced her attention on her watchband.

"I'll let you get back to work then," Beth said and rushed off.

Jo watched her long, tan legs until Beth had disappeared around the corner of the house. What are you doing? she chided herself as she climbed back up on the ladder and savagely attacked the peeling paint. Why are you looking and thinking about her like that? It was just curiosity, Jo decided. Beth Harman was an enigma to her. A single mother running a three-hundred-acre ranch. She glanced across at the clean, well-cared-for outer buildings and the corral where three sleek horses idled in the shade. And she's doing a damn fine job, Jo decided.

Tracy returned several minutes later with a large glass of water. She was wearing a pair of blue shorts and a white cotton top. Amused, Jo watched Tracy's bare toes dig into the grass.

"Mom said I should give you this and then I'm supposed to leave you alone." She held up the glass with both hands. Shelly was still being clutched by one ear.

Jo climbed down from the ladder, grateful for the water. "Thank you," she said.

Tracy watched in silence as Jo gulped the water, then handed the empty glass back to her.

"Do you like kids?" Tracy asked with one eyebrow raised in an inquisitive gaze.

"Sure." Jo climbed back up onto the ladder to escape the conversation as much as to get back to work.

"Mom says I shouldn't bother you because sometimes people don't like kids."

Jo glanced down at her. Tracy was holding the empty glass, clinging to the stuffed dog and trying to block the sun from her eyes. Jo smiled and said, "You don't bother me. But I do have a lot of work to do, so I should get back to it." She saw disappointment cloud Tracy's face. "Maybe you could bring me another glass of water in about an hour. Would you mind doing that? We can talk then while I rest."

"I gotta help clean my room first." Tracy's distaste in the upcoming chore was clearly visible. "I'll tell Mom you need water and come back later." She dashed off, leaving Jo to her work.

The guest room where Jo would be staying was at the end of the hallway. It was small but comfortable with a double bed, a small dresser, and a large overstuffed chair. Most important, it had its own private bath. Jo could hibernate in the room while not working and not have to see anyone. She showered and took her time dressing. She was in no hurry to start the awkward process of sitting through dinner with two people she hardly knew.

When Jo reached the dining room she found Tracy sitting on a chair sniffling and Beth kneeling in front of her with her back to Jo.

"I've told you a hundred times to wear shoes. Now hold still. I'll be as careful as I can," Beth was saying.

Tracy looked up and saw Jo. "I stumped my toe," she sniffed, and a fresh batch of tears threatened.

Beth glanced over her shoulder. "Supper's ready, but we have a minor emergency. I'll only be a second."

"That's fine," Jo said, stepping closer to see what was going on. She grabbed the table for support when she saw the bloody gash on Tracy's big toe.

"Are you all right?" Beth asked, pushing Jo into a chair.

Jo nodded and put her hands over her face in an attempt to block the sight of Tracy's bloody toe as well as to hide her mortification. For as long as she could remember she had grown faint at the sight of someone else's blood. She could cut herself and not flinch, but something about seeing someone else bleeding left her weak-kneed and dizzy.

29

Tracy had forgotten about her toe and was now standing beside Jo patting her arm.

"You must've been in the sun too long today," Beth said, her hand still clinging to Jo's arm.

Jo didn't tell her different. It was less humiliating to let her believe she had been in the sun too long.

"You shouldn't have stayed out so long," Beth said. "I don't want you working tomorrow during the heat of the day."

Jo felt a flicker of irritation. Beth must think she was a total idiot. Someone who didn't know when to get out of the sun. She had been working outside most of her life, and she didn't need Beth Harman telling her when to come in.

"It's not the heat. I wasn't expecting all that blood," she admitted, pulling her hands from her face. The movement forced Beth to withdraw her hand. Jo cringed even more as Tracy and Beth cast dubious glances at the cut.

"It's just a little cut," Tracy said, staring at her.

Yeah, a minute ago you were sniveling and about to bleed to death, Jo thought unkindly. Without thinking, she glanced down at Tracy's toe. A glistening puddle of blood hovered over the cut. Jo felt the familiar sense of lightheadedness, and the room again gave a sickening whirl.

Beth reached out to steady her. "Tracy, why don't you sit over there while I get a bandage for your toe." She pointed to the far side of the table.

"But, Mom, it's only a little cut," Tracy said, holding her foot up and waving it in front of Jo. The movement caused the drop of blood to smear slightly, and Jo averted her gaze.

Tracy giggled. "It's only blood."

Beth's fists went to her hips as she turned to Tracy. "Tracy Janelle Harman, you stop that this minute. How would you have felt if Jo had made fun of you crying over that *little cut*? Now get over to that chair like I told you."

Crestfallen, Tracy did as she was told.

"Are you okay?" Beth asked, still hovering over Jo.

Jo wanted to scream. Hell no I'm not okay. I'm dying of shame. But she decided not to make matters worse. She heard Tracy sniffle. Oh great, I've upset the entire household, and now the poor kid is crying. "I'm fine," she managed to croak out. She wanted to escape to her room, but Beth pushed her back.

"You don't look fine. You stay right here while I get Tracy taken care of." As she walked beside Jo she again placed her hand on her shoulder and this time lightly squeezed it. Jo's stomach gave an odd flip, and a whole new wave of feelings assaulted her nervous system. Maybe I *have* been out in the sun too long, she thought.

Jo and Tracy sat in silence. When Beth returned to the room, she knelt in front of Tracy's chair. They talked quietly as Beth bandaged Tracy's toe.

Jo tried to listen, but they were speaking too low. Embarrassed beyond words, Jo closed her eyes and wanted to disappear. She ran through the gamut of alternatives: She could get up and run from the room. She could go back to San Antonio and never show her face here again. She could move to South America and change her name. A small hand on her arm stopped her silliness. Jo opened her eyes to find a guilty-looking Tracy.

"I'm sorry I made fun of you," Tracy said as big crocodile tears slid down her cheeks.

Jo felt a lump in her own throat. The poor kid looked so pitiful. "I shouldn't be such a wimp," Jo replied, feeling as miserable as Tracy looked. She took one of Tracy's small hands in hers and wiped Tracy's tears away with her free thumb. "I'm sorry too."

"If all the medical emergencies have been sufficiently dealt with, I suggest we eat supper?" Beth said, moving around to stand behind Tracy.

Jo's stomach did another series of flip-flops as her gaze met Beth's and held for a long moment.

31

"Tracy, run and wash your face and we'll eat," Beth said, watching Jo with an intensity that caused Jo's breath to catch.

As Tracy scurried off, Jo forced herself to look away.

"Are you sure you're all right?" Beth asked, her hand again settling on Jo's shoulder and making small circular patterns.

"Except for feeling like a fool, I'm fine," Jo assured her. She tried to ignore the flood of sensations Beth was causing. When the sensations threatened to overflow, she jumped up to escape Beth's hands.

"There's no need to feel bad," Beth assured her. Her hand fell from Jo's shoulder.

Jo realized too late that by standing up she had placed herself in a more precarious position. Beth had not stepped back as Jo had anticipated she would. They now stood only inches apart, and Jo couldn't move away because of the chair and table behind her. It had been a long time since she had been this close to a woman. She could feel the heat that emanated from Beth's body.

She recognized this feeling. Desire. A feeling that she hadn't felt since Diane. Jo was confused. How could she be having these thoughts about someone other than Diane?

For one brief moment Jo was certain she saw the same look of desire in Beth's eyes. Before she could fully analyze it Tracy came bounding into the dining room.

"I'm back," Tracy announced as she skipped to her chair.

Beth stepped away from Jo. "You two sit down, and I'll get the bread from the oven." Without a backward glance she disappeared into the kitchen

Tracy kept up a monologue of chatter during the meal that prevented any uncomfortable pauses in the conversation. Lost in separate thoughts, Jo and Beth answered Tracy's questions in monosyllables.

Jo volunteered to help with the dishes, but Beth declined

the offer. With a sense of relief, Jo excused herself and hid in the solitude of her room. Leaving the lights off, she settled into the large overstuffed chair by the open window and let the cool, night air and sounds wash over her. A chorus of crickets and cicadas provided the low steady background music to the lonely yapping of coyotes. The security light bathed the ranch yard in a soft yellow glow.

She allowed herself to think of nothing but the work she would be doing the following day. By visualizing which areas of the house would be shaded at a particular time, she decided where she would start painting. She made a mental note to replace the short section of trim near the front porch that needed to be repaired.

She listened as the house settled into silence. She heard Beth and Tracy as they prepared for bed. She continued her musing until an owl swept down and perched in regal splendor on the corner of the shed. Mesmerized by the creature's beauty, Jo watched it for several minutes until it took flight and was swallowed by the darkness.

She was left with an overwhelming sense of loneliness and confusion that she couldn't shake. She tried returning to her mental work schedule, but her mind kept returning to Beth and Diane. Her fingers picked at a loose thread on her shorts.

Jo knew she was attracted to Beth. What she didn't understand was how she could be having those feelings when her heart would always belong to Diane.

In less than two weeks it would be the second anniversary of Diane's death. Tears burned Jo's eyes. She sprang from the chair and slipped out into the hallway, which was now dark and silent. Jo eased out the front door and strolled toward the corral. She could see Blossom standing with her head over the rail. Two other horses stood on the opposite side of the corral. Jo ran a cautious hand along Blossom's neck and was rewarded by a soft snuffling sound and a nudge. Climbing onto the rail, she sat in quiet solitude, thinking of nothing but the beauty of the night. Gradually the gentle night breeze and peaceful sounds calmed her enough for her to return to the house and sleep.

Beth heard the soft click of the front door opening. She rose from her bed and went to the window. The corral's security light cast a soft light across the yard, illuminating Jo's tall form as she walked with effortless grace toward the corral. Beth smiled as she saw Jo rub Blossom's neck. She had sensed Jo's fear of horses the day they had ridden to the cabin.

Normally, she would not have intentionally pushed anyone into doing anything they were uncomfortable with, but Jo's air of utter confidence made Beth want to do something that would rattle her. But when she had finally seen Jo rattled, it hadn't been as pleasant as she had thought it would be.

Beth had glanced back to check on her while they were crossing the narrow shelf and had been shocked to see Jo sitting rigid with her eyes clamped shut. Beth had immediately regretted her childish antics.

Beth watched as the strange woman climbed onto the corral railing. She was an intriguing mystery to Beth. One moment Jo was the epitome of confidence, and the next she was fainting over a little blood. And it was a little cut, Beth thought. She giggled before quickly reprimanding herself. She had scolded Tracy for teasing Jo, and here she was doing the same thing.

Beth knew that Tracy was becoming enthralled with Jo. She'd had to tell her a half-dozen times today to leave Jo alone so she could work. Jo seemed to get along with Tracy also. Beth recalled finding them together after she and Tracy had returned from town that morning. Jo had been kneeling on the ground, listening with sincere interest to whatever Tracy had been telling her.

If only Janet and Tracy could get along that well, she thought. But she couldn't start trying to figure out her relationship with Janet; she would be awake for hours. Instead she sat and watched the enigmatic woman who had so confidently strolled into her life. She continued to watch for several minutes more until Jo climbed from the fence and returned to the house.

Beth waited until she heard the soft click of Jo's door closing before she returned to bed. Sleep was slow in coming as she lay thinking about the woman down the hall from her.

Late Friday afternoon, Beth and Ernie were standing by one of the holding pens looking over the cattle. They were choosing which cattle would be sold. Beth glanced up and saw Jo approaching. She knew Jo was probably coming to tell her that the painting was finished. She struggled to think of something else that would keep Jo there. She found the thought of her leaving depressing.

"I'll come back later," Ernie said.

Beth turned to him and caught the flicker of a smile. "What's that smirk all about?" she asked of the man who was more like a father to her than a hired hand. The ranch would not have survived after her father died without the help and support of Ernie and his wife, Wanda.

He gave an exaggerated shrug at her question and turned to leave. "I like her," he said, nodding toward Jo. "And so does Tracy," he added when Beth didn't respond.

Beth felt her face flush. She had never mentioned her sexual preference to Ernie, but she suspected he hadn't been fooled by her tale of Janet renting a room.

"Why don't you *rent* her a room," he added with a wink as he disappeared around the feed shed.

Ernie was forgotten when Beth took in Jo's long confident strides coming toward her. She was dressed in her usual paint-splattered cutoffs, T-shirt, and battered old sneakers. Beth forced her pounding heart to slow down as Jo grew nearer. A large smear of white paint streaked Jo's cheek. Beth slid her hands into her pockets to stop them from reaching out and wiping it off. Why was she finding it so hard to keep from touching this woman?

"I've finished painting," Jo announced.

Beth tried to think of some other repair needed as Jo's gaze settled on the cattle behind Beth.

"If you don't need me for anything else, I thought I'd head back into San Antonio for the weekend."

Beth felt a sharp stab of disappointment. Of course Jo had a life outside of her work. She wouldn't want to spend her weekend here watching them work.

"No, that's fine." She tried to think of something to say. They stood in awkward silence until at last Beth spoke. "Tracy and I will go up to the cabin on Sunday, and you can come up Sunday evening or Monday morning. Whichever is more convenient for you," Beth blurted. For a moment their eyes locked, and Beth felt a stab of sexual desire slice through her. Shocked by her feelings, she looked away. After all, she was committed to trying to make her relationship with Janet work. But Janet had never made her feel this . . . this . . . what?

She couldn't say that her sexual attraction for Jo was stronger than what she felt for Janet. No one would dispute the fact that Janet was a sexually appealing woman.

In fact, in her more truthful moments, Beth often found herself wondering if sex was the only thing between her and Janet. They had never talked about a long-term future together. Their planning was limited to the next time Janet would be in the area.

"I'll need directions to the cabin," Jo said, interrupting her thoughts.

Beth drew her a hasty map on the back of an envelope she had in her pocket. Before Beth could think of an excuse to detain her longer, Jo mumbled good-bye and was gone.

# CHAPTER THREE

Jo drove slowly down Elsie's street admiring the older houses. They had been built in the early 1900s and reflected an era of elegance and grace that Jo found lacking in most modern homes.

She pulled up to a stop sign and attempted to ease some of the weariness in her back by stretching her body over the steering wheel before proceeding. She had spent the day helping Mrs. Smitherton, her eighty-two-year-old neighbor, mow her yard and pull weeds. Jo shook her head and smiled. She had mowed and pulled weeds while Mrs. Smitherton thoroughly briefed her on all the neighborhood gossip. Jo often wondered how Mrs. Smitherton knew so much, since she rarely ventured out her door, and, except for the weekly

Wednesday night visit from her son, no one ever seemed to visit her. A shiver swept through Jo as she thought of growing old alone. She vowed to go over tomorrow and take Mrs. Smitherton to breakfast before leaving for the cabin.

For a moment Jo allowed herself to think about Beth and the feel of Beth's hand on her arm. The memory caused a warmth to spread within her that had nothing to do with the day's heat and humidity. She squirmed and forced her thoughts back to the evening before her.

Elsie had called late last night and invited her for dinner and, as usual, had refused to take no for an answer. Jo pulled into the driveway of the two-story brick home and surveyed the rather plain and unassuming front yard. A privacy fence hid the backyard, but tucked inside the fence was a beautiful rose garden — the true passion of Elsie's life. Jo thought about how much Elsie was like her yard. Her true beauty was always hidden behind a severe and often gruff exterior.

Diane had met Elsie eight years ago while working on a home that Elsie had just sold. They had become fast friends and Diane had invited her over to meet Jo.

At first Jo had been irritated by Elsie's obvious infatuation with Diane. But as time went by and Elsie did nothing to act on her feelings, Jo grew to like, then love this strange woman who strove so hard to keep her passions hidden.

Elsie met Jo at the door with a tall glass of iced tea. At fifty-six Elsie was beginning to show some physical signs of aging. She had more wrinkles and gray hairs with each passing year, but her sharp business aptitude hadn't slipped or softened. Looking up she nailed Jo with deep blue eyes.

"I knew you'd be thirsty after riding across town in that rattletrap you drive. Look at you." She brushed back a lock of Jo's damp hair. "You're burning up. Why don't you buy yourself a decent truck?" She handed the tea to Jo and followed it with a quick hug. Jo knew she was referring to the money that Diane had left her. The money was tucked away in an account that she would never touch. How could she spend money and enjoy life without Diane? Especially money that had come about through Diane's death.

"Come on into the kitchen," Elsie urged. "I'm almost finished."

Jo followed her and shivered when the cold, air-conditioned air swept over her. Elsie kept the temperature of her home at an even sixty-two degrees year-round. Jo sipped her tea, savoring the slight flavor of mint, and wished she had worn slacks. She'd be freezing in ten minutes.

"So tell me all about Beth Harman."

Jo slid onto a stool by the kitchen bar. "What's to tell? She's around my age, maybe a little younger, has a five- or six-year-old daughter, Tracy, and wants a room added onto the cabin." Jo had given Elsie a complete rundown on the job when they spoke on the phone last night.

"But what's she like?" Elsie persisted, ripping lettuce apart into a wooden bowl.

Confused, Jo set her glass down and frowned. "What do you want to know? She seems like a decent sort of person, hardworking, devoted to the kid. What else is there to say?" She's beautiful, gentle, and scares me to death, Jo added to herself.

Elsie paused and looked at her. "You don't remember who she is do you?"

Jo shrugged. "Should I? Is she some kind of celebrity? A daughter or grand-daughter to one of those long-ago politicians or oil millionaires you know?" Jo asked. She was amazed at the number of people Elsie knew. It was a source of constant teasing between them.

Elsie began to dig in the refrigerator. "I've made shrimp kabobs. They're already on the grill and will be ready by the time we finish our salads. Help me set the table."

Jo knew Elsie well enough to know that Beth Harman was a closed subject for now. Elsie needed to think first. She'd get back to the subject in good time, but Jo's interest had been stirred. She struggled to remember if she'd ever heard of Beth Harman.

They ate their meal and discussed the state of the real estate market, and then Elsie gave her a brief update on what their mutual friends were doing. Even though Jo rarely saw any of them, it was nice to hear about how their lives were progressing. But no matter how hard she tried, she couldn't bring herself to join them. They made Diane's absence more pronounced.

After dinner they moved out into Elsie's rose garden to enjoy the soft night air.

Jo made a slow circuit of the garden, stopping often to touch or smell a particular rose that caught her attention. She found it curious that roses had always been so prevalent in her life. Were roses that common? Or did the roses draw her to the people? She ran her hand through her hair. A large yellow rose caught her attention. It had a heavy heady fragrance and brought back the memory of Beth Harman. What was it about the woman? Why was she so attracted to her? Not attracted, Jo reminded herself quickly. She just enjoyed talking to her.

"Nice night," Jo said, directing her attention away from Beth.

"I'm already looking forward to winter," Elsie lamented.

The temperature was still in the mid-eighties, but after Elsie's frigid air conditioning it felt good to Jo.

"You should be a polar bear in your next life," Jo teased.

"With my luck, I'd be captured and sent to the San Antonio Zoo."

Jo chuckled and settled into the chair next to Elsie's. They sat in an easy silence while Elsie sipped a beer and Jo nursed her tea.

"How are you doing?" Elsie's voice was softened by the darkness that surrounded them.

Jo knew she was referring to the impending anniversary

of Diane's death. Elsie was the only person she would discuss Diane with.

"I thought it would be easier this year." She took a long drink of tea to push down the lump that rose in her throat. "About the time I think I have everything under control, I get blindsided by something, a smell, a song, some stupid thing we laughed about. It was hard being around people so much this week."

Jo set the glass on the table beside her and wiped her hands on her shorts. "It's been a rough two years. I wouldn't have made it without you, Elsie. You were always there for me, and I want you to know how much you mean to me."

Elsie set her beer aside. "I knew the minute I saw the two of you together that you had something rare. Diane had a special glow when she was around you or talked about you."

Jo swallowed the persistent lump in her throat and wished they could talk about something else. Could she politely change the subject? How could she tell Elsie that she had spent a lot of time this past week trying not to think about Diane? That she had in fact spent much of her time thinking about another woman? She felt guilty. As if she were in some way being unfaithful to Diane. She knew the thought was ridiculous, but it nagged at her.

Elsie continued, her voice low and strained, "After meeting you I realized how much Diane loved you and that nothing could ever change the way she felt. That she could never love . . ." Elsie's voice broke.

The meaning of her words slammed home. Jo had known almost from the beginning that Elsie was in love with Diane. Jo and Diane had discussed it on a couple of occasions, but they had felt secure enough in their relationship that Elsie wasn't a threat. As they got to know Elsie better, they realized she would never do anything to come between them.

Jo realized she had been selfish in her own grief. Why hadn't she realized how much Elsie had been hurting? Elsie had stood on the sidelines all during Diane's illness, and after

42

her death she had taken care of Jo. But no one had been there for Elsie.

Jo knelt in front of Elsie's chair and hugged her tightly. She couldn't be angry with Elsie now for finally admitting her love for Diane.

"I'm sorry," Jo whispered as Elsie sobbed on her shoulder. "I was so blinded by my own pain, I never thought about yours." She stroked Elsie's short, graying hair.

"Jo, I'm sorry." Elsie sobbed. "I never meant to do this."

"It's all right. I know you loved her too," she whispered. Elsie pulled back and gripped Jo's arms in a frantic grasp.

"After I met you," Elsie murmured, "I knew I could never do anything. If I had, Diane would've hated me." She took a deep breath. "When she got sick, I couldn't tell her . . ." Sobs choked off her sentence.

"She talked about you a lot," Jo said and silently asked Diane to forgive the small lies. Somehow she didn't think Diane would mind if it made their friend feel better. When the sobs grew softer, Jo pulled her chair over and sat next to Elsie.

"I stopped going to the hospital toward the end because I couldn't bare to see her suffering so," Elsie began. "I don't know how you managed to do it. I've always admired your strength." Elsie took the paper towel that had been wrapped around her beer bottle and blew her nose. "I didn't want you to think I had abandoned you both then." She sniffed and rested her head on the back of her chair. "But I guess I did."

Jo reached over to squeeze her arm. The last few days of Diane's life had been such a nightmare for Jo that she hadn't noticed who was or wasn't there. That time frame was just a jumble of doctors, tubes, and Diane's pain. "It's all right. We both understood." They sat without speaking for several moments.

"If you knew I loved her, why didn't you ever say anything to me?" Elsie asked.

It was on the tip of Jo's tongue to tell her that she knew Diane wouldn't allow Elsie to come between them, but it seemed cruel to say so. "You were our friend, and I trusted you not to do anything," Jo answered instead, knowing it was true.

Elsie's soft hand slipped over Jo's callused one and squeezed. They had both lost someone they loved, and being with Elsie made Jo feel better. She made a silent vow not to be so self-centered and to be there for Elsie more in the future.

Later that night as she was drifting off to sleep, Jo realized they had not gotten back to their conversation about Beth Harman.

Beth reached into the darkness for the ringing phone by her bed. It was after eleven, and she didn't want it to wake Tracy.

"Hi," a sultry voice purred when Beth answered.

"Hello, Janet." She experienced the flash of raw sexuality that Janet always caused, but this time it was accompanied by a fleeting moment of disappointment at hearing Janet's voice. Had she been expecting someone else? She pushed aside the vision of the tall woman with wide shoulders and the confident stride.

"Have you thought anymore about our last conversation?" Janet asked.

Beth sat up in bed. Janet had been trying to get her to send Tracy to Dallas to spend the summer with Beth's sister, Karen. "Janet, I can't send her away for the entire summer. I don't mind a week or two weeks, but not the whole summer."

"Not even for me?" Janet's voice lost the silky, sultry tone.

Beth felt her frustration building. She was tired of this ongoing argument. "Why can't we agree to go away together for two weeks? You know it's hard for me to get away from the ranch for that long, but I could leave Ernie in charge and let Tracy stay with Karen."

The silence at the other end sparked a wave of anger in Beth, something that she hadn't before experienced with Janet. The anger made her words seem cold and unrelenting.

"Don't make me choose between you and Tracy. I'm willing to do what I can to make time for us, but I don't intend to send Tracy off somewhere every time you come in. If this is going to work between us, it'll have to include Tracy."

There was only a slight pause before Janet responded. The harsh edge still clung to her words. "I'll be flying into San Francisco tomorrow for two weeks. I'll be staying with Lynn. After that I'm scheduled to go to Los Angeles for a week and then Omaha. I'm trying to trade off Omaha. We'll talk when I get back."

The connection was broken. Beth held the silent phone in her hand. Was Lynn one of Janet's many ex-lovers or a co-worker? The question served to remind Beth how little she knew about Janet. A new suspicion began to pluck at her. Maybe Lynn was a current lover. Had Janet mentioned the name to make Beth jealous? She replaced the receiver on the phone. Shouldn't I be? she wondered.

Beth knew that she'd soon have to reach some compromise with Janet about Tracy. And Tracy about Janet, she added. They had been at odds with each other since the beginning. Beth eased back into bed. It wasn't like Tracy to be so distant toward anyone. Beth wondered if Tracy had somehow sensed her relationship with Janet and was rebelling because of it or if she just sensed Janet's discomfort with her. Either way, Janet was going to have to get over her reluctance to Tracy. Or else.

A long while later, Beth fell into a troubled sleep. She found herself in a long hallway that split off into two corridors: One corridor blasted cold air at her, but at the end of it was a pair of sultry green eyes beckoning her. Beth groaned at the almost painful desire the eyes evoked in her. The air from the other corridor felt warm, and she could barely make out a tall, wide-shouldered form. Beth felt herself being pulled toward the security and warmth.

# CHAPTER FOUR

Jo stood in the tiny kitchen area of the cabin late Sunday afternoon and stared out the window at a pair of sparrows playing on an empty bird feeder. Beth and Tracy had been delayed and had arrived at the cabin only minutes before her and were unpacking the few clothes they brought.

Jo wanted everything ready to begin working early the next morning, so in preparation she went out and set up her sawhorses and a makeshift workbench.

Her conversation with Elsie had left her feeling raw and vulnerable. It had reawakened the memories of the long, anxious hours of waiting in a cold hospital room holding Diane's frail hand. Coming back to haunt her was the paralyzing fear of knowing it was only a matter of time before the life-consuming cancer took Diane, and then the sickening mixture of helplessness and relief that had come with Diane's death.

That was also when the guilt began. Guilt that she was still alive to enjoy the things that Diane loved so much. Guilt at the feeling of relief she had experienced when Diane had finally been released from the weeks of suffering. Guilt that she had spent long hours working before Diane's death, hours they could have spent together.

With the guilt came an anger stronger than any Jo had known. She had grown angry at a world that was so money hungry that it polluted everything it touched. Drinking water that was tainted with dioxides. Air that was poisoned with noxious fumes from hundreds of factories and processors. Food that was filled with life-destroying substances from the hundreds of chemicals pumped into produce and meat-producing animals to make them bigger. And all of this for the sake of profit.

After Diane died, Jo had left the hospital and driven to the dream house they were building on the south side of town. The bare frame of the house seemed to mock all the hopes that were now lost. In a blind rage she had taken a sledge-hammer to the walls before burning them.

The next several months were no more than a blur to her, a distorted series of drunken nightmares and the endless sense of being lost.

Elsie had finally insisted that Jo either give up the alcohol or get out of her life. Elsie proved to be more important, and Jo gave her word that she would try. It had taken her another six months to learn to live without the alcohol, but Elsie stood by her. Jo managed by refusing to allow herself to dwell on the past and by wrapping herself into a tight cocoon of isolation that effectively prevented her from getting close to or involved with anyone.

In accepting this job she had placed herself in the perilous position of spending the next several weeks in close quarters with two people she was already starting to have feelings for. And her feelings were scaring her.

She pulled the ever-present bandanna from her pocket and wiped sweat from her face as she glanced around at the sawhorses and workbench. There was nothing left to set up. Everything was ready for her to begin work. Thirst drove her inside in search of a glass of tea.

Jo took a glass from a small overhead cabinet and glanced around the room. The cabin consisted of two large rooms and a tiny bathroom. The living room/kitchen was a single long area containing a small refrigerator, a stove, and a slightly battered, wooden table and chairs on one side and a worn red vinyl couch and chair with two mismatched end tables on the other. The second room, a bedroom, held two twin beds, a cot, and two chests of drawers that someone had painted a muddy brown.

"Which bed do you want?" Beth called from the bedroom. Jo was tempted to say she would sleep in her truck, but knew she would sound foolish. She walked to the bedroom door and glanced at the setup again.

"That one's fine," she said, pointing to the bed in the farthest corner.

"This one is mine," Tracy announced while bouncing up and down on the cot.

Jo looked at the remaining bed. It was less than four feet away from her own. She was suddenly very relieved that Tracy was with them. Shocked by the turn her thoughts had unwittingly taken, she returned to the kitchen and busied herself with preparing the tea.

Tracy came skipping out of the bedroom behind her. She was singing the catchy little ditty about a spider on a waterspout. Jo tried to recall the words from her own childhood, but they kept slipping away.

"Whatcha doin'?" Tracy asked, plopping Shelly down on the sink beside Jo.

"I'm making some tea. Would you and Shelly like to join me for a glass? Or would she prefer a doggy biscuit?"

Tracy giggled. "Shelly doesn't eat."

"No wonder she's so skinny," Jo teased. She picked up the toy and wiggled it against Tracy's ear, causing her to erupt in another fit of laughter. "Then how about some tea for you?" Jo asked, handing the dog back to Tracy.

"Can I have cookies, too?"

"Shouldn't you ask your mom?"

"Mom, can I have a cookie?" Tracy yelled.

"Only one," Beth called from the bedroom. "They're under the sink."

Kneeling, Jo dug beneath the sink in the well-stocked cabinet. "How did all this food get here?" Jo asked.

"Ernie and I packed it in on horseback yesterday," Beth answered from the bedroom.

Finding a bag of cookies, Jo extracted one and handed it to Tracy. "There you go. One cookie."

"I love you," the child declared, throwing her arms around Jo's neck and hugging her in a tight embrace.

Jo's stomach clutched in a knot as the room gave a crazy spin. Her throat began to close, causing her to breathe in short gasps. She dropped the bag of cookies, pulled away from Tracy, and rushed outside.

The late afternoon air was heavy and humid. It was too late in the day and too hot to be starting anything, but Jo needed to be busy. Grabbing an armload of two-by-fours, she went to work. The smell of the fresh lumber and the familiar feel of hammer and saw soon cleared her mind of everything but the work in front of her.

Jo was cutting a new stack of supports when Beth brought her a glass of tea. Unwilling to face the conversation that she suspected was coming, Jo continued to saw until Beth finally gave up, set the tea down, and went back inside. As she continued to work, Jo managed to place Tracy's feelings into a perspective that she could handle. After all, Tracy was only a child. She would be drawn to anyone who showed her any attention. When the room was finished and Jo returned to San Antonio, Beth and Tracy would be nothing more than a fond memory. There were no permanent attachments here to fear, she told herself.

It was almost dark when Jo carefully wiped off her tools and placed them back inside her truck. She wasn't ready to go inside and face them yet. She knew she would have to apologize to Tracy, but she needed a few more minutes. She decided to explore the area around the cabin, and her rambling path took her to the river. She stood at the edge and stared down the gradual slope to the water. It would be a great place to swim. Maybe she'd have time to swim later in the week.

She was so lost in thought that she failed to notice Beth until she was beside her.

"This is one of my favorite spots," Beth said. "When I was a kid my dad would bring me here to fish."

"It's peaceful," Jo mumbled, uncomfortable with Beth's closeness.

Beth turned to face Jo. "I know kids can be annoying if you're not used to being around them, but Tracy's really upset. She thinks you're angry with her."

Jo continued to stare across the river. She regretted having hurt Tracy's feelings, but she didn't want anyone to like her, and she didn't want to love anyone. It was too easy to lose people you loved. Ultimately, love hurt too much. This is precisely the reason why she shouldn't have taken this job. After only a week she already felt a strong attachment to Beth and Tracy, and it scared her. She sensed Beth was waiting for her to say something, but she didn't know how to explain.

Finally, Beth gave up and turned back toward the cabin. "Be careful where you step. We've killed several rattlesnakes up here."

When she was alone again, Jo ran her hands through her hair and sighed. Rattlesnakes didn't scare her nearly as much as her budding feelings for Beth Harman.


Beth was at the sink making a cucumber salad when Jo came in. She was careful not to turn to look at Jo as she passed by. A moment later she heard the shower come on. Beth shook her head and wondered again if she had made a mistake in hiring this woman who was already disrupting their lives. Jo's abrupt departure had upset Tracy so badly she had gone to bed without supper. Beth didn't kid herself. She was attracted to the tall, silent woman who had walked with such confidence into their lives.

This thought made her think of Janet. The only reason she had even considered adding a room onto the cabin was because of Janet's constant complaining that she and Beth never had any privacy. Beth rubbed her temples where a headache threatened. Privacy with a six-year-old child around was difficult.

She thought about Janet's demand that Tracy spend the entire summer away from home. Beth didn't mind Tracy staying with Karen for a couple of weeks while she and Janet got away, but not for the entire summer. She hoped that adding a room onto the cabin would show Janet she was trying to arrange ways to give them more privacy without making Tracy feel like she was being pushed aside. When Janet returned they needed to sit down and discuss ways the three of them could spend time together. Well, if she returns, she thought, thinking of their disastrous conversation the previous night.

Janet was a software training consultant, and her job entailed a great deal of traveling. They had met when Janet, who was in town visiting a client, backed her car into Beth's at the mall. Beth had felt an immediate sexual attraction to her.

Two days later, she had shown up at the ranch. Tracy was at school, and Beth and the hired hands were repairing the hay shredder and getting things ready to start baling hay.

When Beth heard the crunching of tires on the gravel of the driveway, she had gone to see who it was. She was surprised when she walked around the corner of the house to find the attractive woman who had backed into her truck at the mall.

Beth's truck hadn't sustained any damage, but the car had a rather nasty dent on its rear bumper. She instantly assumed the woman was there in response to the accident. As her eyes wandered over the woman's sleek form, Beth again experienced the exciting tingle of desire race through her.

"Hello," Janet called as she strolled up the walkway. "I hoped I'd be able to find you at home."

Beth gave a small wave. "How did you know where to find me? This isn't the easiest place to locate."

Janet spread her hands. "It was simple. I tracked down the mail carrier and asked him."

"Resourceful."

Janet gave a wicked smile that made Beth's breath catch. "That's me. Resourceful."

"What can I do for you?" Beth asked, trying to control her hormones.

"Well, since I've already admitted to tracking you down, I guess it's too late to say I was just in the neighborhood and decided to stop by."

"I would say so," Beth agreed.

Janet raised her hands, palms up, and shrugged. "In that case, I'm forced to admit that I'm attracted to you and wanted to see you again."

Too shocked to respond, Beth could only stare.

"Have I shocked you?" Janet asked, taking a step closer.

Beth slid her hands into the hip pockets of her faded jeans before giving a nervous laugh. "I believe you have," she admitted.

"I'm not mistaken in your inclination, am I?"

Beth hesitated. She had discovered her lesbian tendencies while in college and had had a couple of brief affairs with women before she'd met Mark. Her attraction to him had left her confused and uncertain. He was so completely different from anyone she had ever known. She found his rebel ways both dangerous and exciting. Her marriage to him had been the biggest mistake of her life.

Mark had been her last lover, and that had been over six years ago. Too many things had been going on in her life for her to give much thought to her sexuality. There had been the horrible weeks during the trial, followed by her father's death. Beth had been numb with grief. A few months later, Tracy was born and Beth found herself having to cope not only with the demanding responsibilities of the ranch but also with a baby as well.

She realized Janet was waiting for an answer. She shook her head. "No, I don't think you've made a mistake."

Janet looked surprised. "You don't think. Does that mean you're not sure?"

Beth thought for a second. "No, it means that it's not a subject I've really given much thought to in a long time."

Janet stepped closer. "Maybe it's time to start thinking about it again."

Beth shook her head. "You don't waste any time, do you?"

"Time is too precious to waste. I believe in living every minute like it's my last. And right now, I'm very attracted to you and want to get to know you much better."

Beth, not knowing what to say, hesitated, trying to find a way out of an awkward situation.

Janet rushed in to fill the silence. "Show me around. I've never been on a real Texas ranch." She walked to Beth and took her arm. "Show me the horses first. I love horses."

Beth knew horses and was comfortable talking about them. They walked to the corral, and Beth called the horses to the fence. Janet insisted they go for a ride, and before long they were racing across the pastures. Beth guided them to the big oak tree that was located in the corner of the ranch. It was a nice secluded area, and Beth would later wonder about her choice of direction. Had she deliberately chosen this spot because of its seclusion?

Janet reined in beneath the massive tree and hopped from the horse. "My god," she said in awe, "what a beautiful tree."

"It's been here since before the Harmans purchased this land," Beth informed her. "No one really knows how old it is." She stepped down from the saddle and took Janet's reins.

Janet walked around the tree while Beth tied the horses and loosed their cinches. Janet hadn't reappeared from the far side of the tree, so Beth went to find her. As she stepped around the tree, Janet's arm reached out and pulled Beth to her.

"I really don't want to waste what little time we have making small talk about the plant life."

Beth felt hypnotized by Janet's green eyes.

"Please tell me you're not going to insist on wasting this wonderful afternoon with coy chitchat," Janet said.

Beth answered by kissing Janet. Beth knew that she was being irresponsible and that it was a ridiculous thing to be doing. She knew nothing about this woman, and somehow that made the entire liaison that much more exciting. Beth moaned with pleasure when Janet's hands caressed Beth's side.

"Yes," Janet cooed. "My little cowgirl is ready." She tugged Beth's shirt from the faded jeans while her lips explored the dips and curves of Beth's neck.

Desperate to feel Janet's bare skin against her, Beth reached for Janet's shirt buttons.

Janet stopped her. "Not yet," she whispered. "First things first." She pushed Beth against the oak tree and slowly unbuttoned Beth's shirt. In one smooth move she plucked away Beth's bra. "Very nice," Janet praised. "Just like I knew they would be." Her hands cupped Beth's breasts. When she gently squeezed the swollen nipples, Beth cried out in pleasure.

"You are ready, aren't you?" Janet murmured before taking a nipple into her mouth.

Janet moved hungrily from one breast to the other until Beth was begging for release. Janet released the button and the zipper on Beth's jeans.

In desperation Beth pushed the pants from her hips and tried to kick them off, but the legs tangled over her boots.

Janet's foot slipped between Beth's and pushed Beth's legs apart as far as the tangled jeans would allow. Beth tried to struggle out of them, but Janet stopped her.

"Be still," Janet commanded.

Beth stopped struggling, and Janet's fingers slid between Beth's legs and pushed into her dripping passion.

"Ohh," Janet moaned. "My little cowgirl is definitely ready. You are ready, aren't you baby?" Janet asked.

"Yes," Beth panted.

"Tell me," Janet insisted.

"I'm ready," Beth repeated.

"For what?" Janet teased, while slowly sliding her fingers through Beth's creamy juices.

"Take me. Please. Now," she was practically screaming.

"Yes," Janet replied, and let her tongue trace the edge of Beth's ear. Without warning, Janet's weight shifted and pinned Beth to the tree, while her fingers slid deep into Beth.

Janet pushed deeper and gave a loud moan, sending Beth over the edge of a throbbing, pulsating abyss of pleasure. Beth pushed herself against Janet's hand again and again. The rough bark of the tree dug into her bare skin, but Beth couldn't stop. Her hands closed around Janet's hips and pulled her tightly against her. Just when Beth was sure she couldn't stand anything more, Janet pushed her to her knees and knelt behind her.

Beth screamed when Janet slid her fingers back inside her and with the other hand began to almost savagely stroke her. The world went crazy for Beth. She was oblivious to everything but the feel of Janet's hands. She lost track of the number of times she came, and later she couldn't remember how she had ended up on her back with Janet kneeling over her face. She only remembered her frantic need to taste Janet. The burning need to bury her tongue again and again deep inside Janet's delicious center.

The sun had been low in the western sky before Janet and Beth made it back to the ranch.

Beth had not been worried about Tracy coming home from school because she knew Ernie would be there until she returned. If he had something to do and had to leave, he would simply leave Beth a note and take Tracy home with him. Ernie and Wanda were like grandparents to Tracy.

Tracy came running to meet them. "Mom," Tracy yelled as Beth slid from her horse. "I found a nickel on the playground today that had a buffalo on it. Miss Ruiz said it was real old, but we couldn't see the date because it was too old and dirty. Ernie put it in water for me so we can clean it."

Beth knelt, and Tracy threw her arms around Beth's neck. "That's great, sweetie. We'll look at it together in a little while, okay?" Beth picked Tracy up and swung her onto the horse's back. "Tracy, this is my friend, Janet." Beth looked at Janet as she tugged on Tracy's bare toes. "And this little barefooted chatterbox is my daughter, Tracy."

Janet stepped down from her horse. "Hello, Tracy."

"Hi. Do you want to see my buffalo nickel?" Tracy asked.

"No, thanks." Without bothering to look at Tracy, Janet began to stroke the horse's neck.

Beth felt herself grow warm thinking about what those hands had been doing to her such a short time before. Flustered, she took the reins of Janet's horse and handed them up to Tracy.

"Sweetie, will you take the horses into the barn and ask one of the guys to unsaddle them? I'll be along soon to rub them down."

"Okay." Tracy turned the horses and kicked her mount into a light trot.

Janet stood looking after her. "I didn't know you had a daughter."

Beth arched her eyebrows. "We haven't exactly spent much time talking."

Janet gave her a look that made Beth's legs weak. "Why talk when there are so many other much more pleasant things to do?" She stepped forward and pulled Beth into her arms.

Beth stepped away and turned to see where Tracy was. She was relieved to see Tracy had already disappeared inside the barn.

"What's wrong?" Janet asked, a frown creasing her forehead.

"Nothing. I'd just prefer to be a little more discreet around Tracy and the guys who work for me."

"Why? She's a kid, and the hired hands work for you. If they don't like it let them work somewhere else."

Surprised by her attitude, Beth started to reply. But Janet stopped her by holding up her hands.

"Listen to me." She stepped a safe distance from Beth. "I'm sorry. I spend so much time traveling and dealing with so many different people that I forget how the real world is. Forgive me?" She tilted her head and smiled sweetly at Beth. "Give me a chance to redeem myself. Have dinner with me tomorrow night. I have to fly to Phoenix the following day, and it'll be at least three weeks before I can get back to San Antonio."

Beth almost agreed, before she remembered she had already made plans with Tracy. "I can't. Tracy's school is having an open house tomorrow night, and I've already promised Tracy we would go."

"But I'm leaving for three weeks. Surely Tracy would understand," Janet pleaded.

"I'm sorry, but I promised her."

A shadow crossed Janet's face so quickly that Beth wondered if she had imagined it. Janet took a step closer to Beth and lowered her voice. "I can't wait three weeks to taste you again. Let me stay the night."

Beth started to say no, but Janet slid a finger into her mouth and sucked it gently. Beth's breath caught at the sight. Just a short time earlier those fingers had been plunging into her, making her beg for release.

The lust-driven part of her was screaming yes, while common sense told her to slow down. Apparently lust was the stronger of the two factors, because she heard herself agreeing.

Things had gone fairly well for them during those first few months. Janet was never in town for more than a couple of days each month, and it was always during the week while Tracy was in school. The friction between Janet and Tracy started when school broke for summer vacation and Tracy was home when Janet arrived. Janet immediately began to resent the fact that Beth couldn't just ride away or disappear behind a bedroom door for hours when Tracy was there. To make matters worse, Janet and Tracy couldn't get along. Maybe it was jealousy on both their parts, Beth reasoned.

The shower shut off, snapping Beth back from her daydreaming. A few minutes later Beth heard the bathroom door open. She set the salad on the table and removed the roast from the Crock-Pot. She would have to go and try to convince Tracy to eat.

As she approached the bedroom door, she heard Tracy's voice.

"So you're not mad at me?"

"No. I'm not mad. Sometimes adults get a little cranky."

"Like Mom is after Janet leaves?" Tracy asked.

Beth felt her face flame. What would Jo think?

"Everybody does now and then," Jo answered. "Don't you ever just get sad sometimes?"

Beth's pulse quickened as she studied the outline of Jo's body sitting on the edge of Tracy's cot. Her back was to Beth.

"Yeah. Why are you so sad?"

Beth knew she should call them to supper and save Jo from Tracy's questions, but she wanted to hear Jo's answer. What had placed that veil of sadness in Jo's eyes?

Beth could hear the struggle in Jo's voice before it dropped so low she had to strain to hear.

"Someone very special to me died."

"Was it your dog? Cause I was real sad when Buster died."

"I'm sure you were," Jo said standing abruptly. "We'd better go eat before your mom decides we're not hungry and throws everything out. I'm starved."

"Me too."

Beth backed away from the doorway. She was busy setting the table when Jo and Tracy came into the kitchen. Tracy was holding Jo's hand.

For once Beth was grateful for Tracy's nonstop chatter throughout the meal. She gave automatic responses to Tracy's questions and thought about the woman across the table from her. She had to be a dyke. Beth had determined that the first time she saw Jo standing on her front porch. No straight woman could carry herself with that kind of confidence, that easy self-assurance and comfortable knowledge of one's body. Why did Jo intrigue her so? she wondered.

Since she was in love with Janet, should she be spending so much time thinking of Jo? Was she in love with Janet or in lust with her? That question made her nervous. Janet's the reason you're up here adding on a room, she reminded herself. If she didn't care for Janet would she be going to all this trouble and expense? Then an odd thought struck her. If Janet hadn't left, I would never have met this woman. For a tiny second Beth was glad Janet had gotten upset and left. She quickly banished the thought. After all, she was committed to making her relationship with Janet work. Wasn't she?

# CHAPTER FIVE

By late Wednesday afternoon Jo was ready to raise the first section of the outer wall frame. To ensure that Tracy was safely out of the way, Beth had sent her off to play. Together Jo and Beth managed to lift the wall frame. They were securing it to the cabin when Beth's hammer slipped and scraped across Jo's hand.

"Oh gosh. I'm sorry," Beth apologized, as Jo's skinned knuckle began to bleed.

"It's okay," Jo replied, pulling a clean, blue bandanna from her pocket and wrapping it tightly around the scrape. "I do it all the time. It's an occupational hazard."

Beth's hand was on Jo's arm, and she was watching her closely. "Do you need to sit down?"

Confused, Jo stared at her before realizing Beth was afraid she was going to faint. Blushing, she shook her head. "It's only someone else's blood that bothers me."

"Oh. Well, let me put something on it anyway."

"It's fine," Jo called, but Beth had already disappeared around the corner. Jo removed the bandanna and finished securing the retaining nails.

"Here." Beth was back with a bottle of antiseptic and an adhesive bandage.

Feeling somewhat silly, Jo held out her hand. Beth sprayed the cut and began to blow on it. A wave of sexual desire slammed into Jo so strongly she gasped.

"I'm sorry it burns," Beth said, misinterpreting Jo's reaction.

Seemingly on their own, Jo's fingers curled around Beth's. The world seemed to stop. Jo focused her attention on Beth's neck. She watched the throbbing of Beth's pulse and leaned forward slightly to inhale the delicate scent of roses. Logic was telling her to let go of Beth's hand, but her body was telling her to do much more.

"Mom! Jo!" Tracy screamed from the direction of the river. Jo dropped Beth's hand, and both women rushed off toward the sound. Tracy was down near the edge of the river. She was on her knees and scrunched forward into a tight ball. Jo recalled Beth's warning about rattlesnakes and ran faster.

"Tracy!" Beth yelled as she sped past Jo and slid to a stop on her knees beside Tracy.

"Look!" A radiantly happy Tracy held up a baby rabbit.

A wave of conflicting emotions flooded Jo as she realized Tracy was safe.

"Why did you scream like that?" Beth demanded, her face ghostly pale.

"I wanted to show you what I'd found," Tracy mumbled, looking back and forth between the women.

"Tracy, you nearly scared me to death. I thought you'd stepped on a rattlesnake or something," Beth said. She turned her back and wrapped her arms around her chest, but not soon enough to hide her tears.

On seeing her mother's tears, Tracy's own began. "I'm sorry," she sniffed. "I just wanted to show you and Jo the baby rabbit."

Jo gave Beth's arm a quick squeeze before kneeling by Tracy and giving her a hug.

"I wanted you to see," Tracy declared, looking at Jo.

"We know. You scared us, though." She brushed the hair from Tracy's face. "Show us what you found."

Tracy kept staring at her mother.

"Give her a second and she'll be all right," Jo whispered to the child. "Where'd you find this little guy?" she asked, running a shaking finger along the rabbit's back. Tracy's scream had scared her. A part of her was thankful for the interruption Tracy had caused, but on some level she was also a little disappointed. She would have to wait until later to sort out what could have happened had Tracy not interrupted them. She took several deep breaths to calm her hammering heart while Tracy began to explain her discovery.

"He was right there," Tracy answered, still torn between watching her mother and explaining her prize find.

"He looks kind of scared," Jo said, picking up the rabbit and cradling it in her hands while Tracy ran a cautious finger between its ears. Jo looked up to find Beth watching her. She swallowed the ache of desire in her throat and tried to control the new wave of trembling that took over her hands.

Beth knelt beside Tracy, kissed the top of her head, and pulled her into a tight embrace. Jo held the rabbit closer to them so they could both pet it. She tried to focus on the rabbit and ignore the flash of fire that shot through her each time Beth's skin came in contact with her own.

"Can I keep it?" Tracy asked, staring up at Beth.

"I don't think you should," Beth answered, cupping Jo's hand in her own.

"Its mother's probably close by," Jo managed to choke out

around her ragged breathing, her gaze locking with Beth's. "We should leave it where you found it, and she'll come for it."

Reluctantly Tracy gave in, and Beth removed her hand. Jo placed the small creature on the ground, and the three of them returned to the cabin. While Beth and Tracy went for a walk to work out what had happened down by the river, Jo began to pound another wall frame together. What the hell am I doing? she wondered. She recognized the wild array of feelings that were coursing through her body. It's been two years, she found herself reasoning. Of course she could still be sexually attracted to a woman. But I'm not! she fumed. How could I be? There's only Diane. Besides, I have no desire to get involved with anyone ever again.

Jo had loved Diane so much and still couldn't save her, forced to sit helplessly by while Diane suffered with the horrible pain. She hadn't even been able to give her the one thing Diane had asked for.

Diane had been a hopeless romantic. She would cry over mushy greeting card commercials and sappy movies. She had first mentioned a commitment ceremony about a year after they moved in together. She didn't want just a few friends over for the event. She insisted they invite both of their families. Jo didn't even want to discuss the idea. She didn't believe in commitment ceremonies.

Jo would never forget the last time Diane had broached the subject. They had just celebrated their eighth anniversary and had flown to Dallas for the weekend. On the flight back Diane had placed her head on Jo's shoulder and murmured, "Looks like we survived the seven year itch. Will you marry me, now?"

Jo didn't want to have the conversation again and tried to divert it. "We don't need to have a ceremony. We already have a toaster, two can openers, and more bath towels than we can store."

Diane gave a small sigh. "Jo, it's not about receiving gifts. I want everyone to know how much I love you. A ceremony is a way to celebrate our commitment to each other."

Jo felt a flicker of irritation. They'd had a wonderful weekend, and Diane was going to ruin it by nagging her about the ceremony again. And no matter how Jo tried to ease around the subject, they always ended up arguing about it.

"Diane, you know I love you and I know you love me. Why do we have to have a ceremony to tell everyone? It's nobody's business. Besides, people have commitment ceremonies and break up a year later. What's the point?"

Diane sat up and gazed out the window for a few seconds before speaking. "Are you ashamed to tell your parents about me?"

"No."

"Then why haven't you? Jo, we've been together for eight years, and the only time I've met them was when they made an unscheduled stop in San Antonio and surprised you. You go to St. Louis to see them once a year and you've never invited me to go. Why not?"

"You'd be bored," Jo answered. She put the magazine she had been flipping through aside. "I've told you before. When I go see my parents, we sit around the house all day. Mom and Dad tell me all about what's been going on in the family since I talked to them last, and then we discuss what's been happening with the neighbors. That usually takes about an hour, maybe two.

"The rest of the time I'm there we watch television or Mom and I work in her garden. Dad asks me about the business and we spend a lot of time cursing the weather and politicians. You wouldn't have any fun." Jo and her parents were close, but they seldom engaged in heart-to-heart, parent-to-child conversations. She knew her parents seemed to confide everything to each other, but she had never felt comfortable with that kind of sharing.

Jo realized early on that Diane needed her to be more vocal and expressive about her feelings, and had tried hard. Over the years, she had learned to feel comfortable openly sharing her feelings with Diane. But she still saw no need to share them with her family and friends. What was the purpose of a conventional wedding ceremony? she'd argued. A couple stated their intention of commitment to the State and to the church. So it seemed meaningless to Jo to hold a ceremony that wasn't recognized by the State or the church. She took Diane's hand. "You know I could never be ashamed of you. Please don't think that. I'm just trying to make things easier for you. My parents would bore you."

Diane rubbed her temple.

"Are you getting another headache?" Jo asked.

"Yeah." Diane began to dig through her bag for a pain reliever.

The headaches were getting more frequent and more intense. "You should see a doctor. You may need to have your eyes examined."

"I called Friday morning and made an appointment with Dr. Stone. She's going to work me in next week. I guess I forgot to mention it in all the excitement of packing to leave," Diane said.

Jo took a pillow from the overhead bin and gave it to her. "Why don't you try to sleep for a while? Maybe that will help."

Diane gave a small snort. "You just want me to go to sleep so I won't nag you anymore."

Jo grinned. "Guilty as charged." She placed a hand on Diane's cheek. "I love you more than life itself. But my private life is private. I don't want it displayed for the whole world."

Diane took the pillow. "Do you really feel that strongly about it?"

"Yes."

Diane gazed at her and finally sighed. "All right. I won't bring it up again."

Jo relaxed, and Diane tucked the pillow against the side of the plane and curled up against it.

"At least not until our ninth anniversary," Diane said, tossing Jo a wicked smile.


The sound of Tracy's laughter floated up from the river, snapping Jo from her reverie. She realized she had been holding a two-by-four and staring into space, lost in memories of Diane.

She dropped the board and went for a walk in the opposite direction from where Tracy and Beth were. She wandered until she came upon a small stand of young oak trees. She found a nice patch of grass in the shade of one of the trees and sat down.

Diane had died before their ninth anniversary, and she had asked Jo one last time for the ceremony. As Diane's condition grew worse, Jo finally gave in. She called her parents on two separate occasions with the intention of telling them, but both times she had been unable to say the words. She told Diane they could hold the ceremony without her parents, but Diane had shaken her head and told Jo no. She would wait until everyone could be there. She had died before Jo found the courage to talk to her parents, but not before Diane had made one final request of Jo.

"Tell your parents. I know they love you and will support you. Don't go through this alone."

Jo had promised Diane she would try, knowing even as she uttered the promise that she wouldn't be able to honor it. Diane had gone into a coma a few short hours later and the promise was forgotten.

Jo began to question her reasons for not telling her parents. She had never thought of herself as being "in the

68

closet." She just hadn't seen the need to tell everyone. But not being able to tell her parents about her true feelings about Diane, about Diane's illness and eventual death, made Jo sit down and analyze her reasoning. It occurred to her that she felt like she had let her parents down. They had worked so hard to give her everything, and she didn't feel she had given them anything in return.

In her junior year, Jo's high school guidance counselor had told Jo's parents that she possessed a high aptitude for math and the sciences. Somewhere in the conversation the word *doctor* had been uttered, and for weeks Jo's mother had stopped everyone she knew on the streets and in the grocery store to tell them that her Jo was going to be a doctor. Jo had deliberately let her math and science grades slip until her mom stopped talking about medical school.

As graduation grew nearer her parents started pressuring her to go to college, but she had refused. She wanted to be a carpenter like her father. At the time, she was sure this would please him. But on the day he signed the papers giving her full control over Merrick Construction, he had tears in his eyes when he said, "JoJo, I always thought I'd be able to give you more." Jo had assumed at the time that he simply meant he was sorry the business wasn't larger, but later she would wonder.

When Jo was young her parents had made a few subtle comments about grandchildren, but by the time Jo reached thirty the comments had stopped.

She knew her parents loved her. That was the one certainty in her life after Diane's death. In time she grew to realize that she had been unable to tell them because she couldn't bare the thought of disappointing them again.


The work on the room continued to progress on schedule. Jo stored her feelings for Beth and evaded any possibility of being alone with her. They fell into an easy routine. On Saturday mornings, Jo drove back to San Antonio while Beth and Tracy returned to the ranch.

Jo discovered she was going to be alone on the following Saturday, the second anniversary of Diane's death. Elsie's sister in Vermont had taken ill, and Elsie had flown up to be with her. Elsie explained she would be gone at least two weeks and perhaps longer and apologized for not being there with Jo.

As the date drew nearer, Jo felt the pressure of facing the lonely weekend. She was going to have to face her demons alone without the aid of alcohol or work to deaden the pain.

Friday afternoon she made up her mind to stay at the cabin and work. She decided not to tell Beth, fearing Beth would feel compelled to stay and help her.

Jo remained in bed Saturday morning as long as Tracy's bounding energy would permit and then slowly dressed. Beth and Tracy were ready to leave by the time she sat down for coffee.

Jo had noticed a change in Beth's attitude toward her since the day by the river. Perhaps sensing Jo's hesitation, Beth had become distant as well. She was now careful not to touch Jo when they worked, and if she did bump into her she would apologize. There were times when her aloofness left Jo feeling hurt and confused, until she remembered that she was supposed to be avoiding Beth.

"I'll clean up the dishes before I leave," Jo promised as Beth packed the last of Tracy's and her dirty laundry. Jo reminded herself that she would have to rinse her own clothes out in the sink if she wanted clean underwear next week.

"All right. I'm going to go ahead and leave then. Tracy, grab some of this stuff."

Jo picked up the bag of laundry and followed them out. She stood quietly by and watched while Beth saddled the horses.

"Make sure you lock the door when you leave," Beth reminded her.

"I will," Jo promised and wondered why Beth bothered to lock the door. No one would ever be able to find the place. She'd had trouble finding it the first time with a map.

"We'll see you tomorrow evening then," Beth said with a small, crooked smile that caused Jo's breath to catch.

Tracy gave Jo a quick hug before allowing Beth to help her into the saddle. With a final wave and a chorus of good-byes from Tracy, they were soon out of sight.

Jo returned to the cabin for her coffee and sat on the cool, shaded porch until memories began to invade and she set off to work.

The room would soon be finished, and Tracy and Beth would be out of her life. She felt an odd sense of loss but brushed it aside. She found herself wondering about Janet and about Beth's ex-husband. Tracy never talked about her father, and Beth never spoke of either of them.


The blazing sun climbed high into the sky, but Jo worked on. The hammering and sawing gave her the physical relief she needed to keep her memories at bay. As the sun slipped deep in the west she put away her tools and walked toward the river. The water level was higher than it had been. That meant it was raining somewhere upstream or downstream. Jo could never remember which way that logic went. Maybe the rain will move this way, she thought with a surge of hope. The cool ripples looked so inviting that she stripped off her clothes and waded in. The water felt good rippling across her body. She swam until she grew tired and then flipped onto her back and floated. She let her mind wander as freely as her body.

"Long cup of coffee," Beth's voice called from the bank.

Jo slipped her body below the water. "Hi," she squeaked,

startled by Beth's sudden appearance. Beth was standing on the edge of the bank holding Jo's clothes. Jo, realizing how silly she must look trying to hide in the water, swam toward Beth. She cursed the extra daylight the long summer days provided. This wouldn't be so awkward in the dark. If it had been almost anyone other than Beth Harman, Jo would not have been so conscious of her nakedness. But there was something about the way Beth stood looking at her that made Jo uncomfortable. She was surprised when Beth stepped back as Jo got out of the water.

She's trying to intimidate me, Jo realized. Determined not to let her insecurities show, Jo squared her shoulders, strode up the riverbank, and, as casually as possible, took her clothes from Beth's hands. Trying to prove she wasn't flustered by Beth's presence, Jo didn't turn away as she stepped into her shorts and pulled her shirt over her head.

"So is it Sunday already?" she asked, conscious that Beth was still watching her. She pushed her wet hair away from her face and squeezed as much of the water as she could from it.

"No," Beth said. "Tracy starts back to school on Monday, so I drove by Wanda's to see if she could keep Tracy during the week until we finish the room. Tracy loves to stay with Wanda and Ernie. While I was standing there talking to Wanda and feeling really crappy about leaving Tracy for the whole week, Tracy spied Wanda and Ernie's new puppy. She decided she'd like to start her vacation with them today rather than tomorrow. So I came back up here to lick my parental wounds in solitude.

"And I've spoiled it for you. I can leave." Jo felt a sharp stab of disappointment; she didn't want to return to her empty house in San Antonio.

"There's no need for you to leave. If I'm disturbing you, I'll go. You're welcome to use the cabin."

Jo turned from Beth's intense gaze. "No, I just decided to stay and work since everything's been going so well. I want to get the room closed in before the rain starts."

Beth looked at the sky longingly. "Do you suppose it'll ever rain again? It's been so long I've almost forgotten what it looks like."

"The river's rising, so it must be raining somewhere."

They strolled back to the cabin and stood for an awkward moment trying not to stare at each other. Without Tracy to guide the conversation, there seemed to be nothing to say.

"I need a shower," Jo blurted and disappeared into the bathroom.

When she emerged Beth was standing in the doorway looking out into the darkness. "I brought a six-pack up with me. It's in the refrigerator if you'd like one." She took a long drink of the beer she was holding. "I've moved a couple of the kitchen chairs outside. I thought it might be nice to sit out there for a while."

I'll stay long enough to drink one glass of tea and then I'll go home, Jo told herself. "Sounds good," she replied. What she really wanted to do was sneak back down to the solitude of the river. Instead she poured herself a glass of tea and followed Beth outside. The moon was only a sliver, and the stars winked seductively from a billion miles away.

"Do you not drink at all, or do you not like beer?" Beth asked as Jo settled into her chair.

Jo took a deep breath. It never got easier for her no matter how many times she had to say it. "I'm an alcoholic. I can't drink." She prepared herself for the usual barrage of questions.

"I admire your self-control. I've never been able to curb myself. I always jump in with both feet and suffer or enjoy the consequences."

"For me it's not a matter of self-control," Jo said. "It's survival."

"Survival I can understand." Beth gave a soft sigh. "Tracy was my reason to survive."

Jo heard the soft quiver in her voice and realized Beth was crying. "You're missing her, aren't you?"

73

Beth wiped her eyes with the back of her hands. "I'm being silly. You probably think I'm another one of those clinging mothers."

"Not really. The truth is, I kind of miss the little chatterbox myself."

Beth turned to look at her. The light from the cabin reflected her proud smile. "She can run on, can't she? With her constant jabbering we've hardly had a chance to talk." She tilted her head. "I don't even know you."

To lighten the mood Jo stood and made a formal display of extending her hand. "Hello, I'm Jo Merrick."

Beth took her hand and responded with some flippant remark, but Jo missed it. She was too busy trying to control the flames of desire that consumed her when Beth's smooth hand closed around hers. Their gaze met and held. Neither of them spoke as Jo began to gently glide her thumb back and forth across the back of Beth's hand. Let go of her hand, Jo's mind screamed, but her muscles refused to obey. Beth rose from the chair.

Jo was vaguely aware of the sound of Beth's beer bottle hitting the ground, and then Beth's free hand was on Jo's waist. Jo's body burned with a heat as hot as a Texas August sun. Beth's lips were inches from her own, her breasts pressing against Jo's, her hand burning a path up Jo's back.

Jo's free hand came up to caress Beth's face. Beth's eyes closed to accept Jo's kiss. Warm, soft lips pressed Jo's. Lips that were so similar, yet so different. Her body began to respond, and suddenly Diane's face loomed before her.

"No!" Jo yanked away and tripped over her chair. Beth's hand shot out to steady her, but Jo pulled away. "I'm sorry," she blurted, turning and running to her truck.


It was well after midnight before she reached San Antonio. With Elsie out of town, there was no one else she could call.

She had pushed away all of her friends so many times that they had finally given up and stopped trying to contact her. It was too late to call her parents. Besides, they would only chat about the weather or spend the time telling her about other family members.

She paced the distance of her tiny living room and kitchen. An irrational part of her screamed that she had betrayed Diane's memory. How could she even think of kissing another woman? At the same time, another part of her taunted her. You're scared of making another commitment. It was this part of her that kept recalling the feel of Beth's lips against her own.

For the first time in over a year she wanted a drink. Her approach to avoiding alcohol was work. Alcoholics Anonymous and the other support groups hadn't worked for her. She had never been able to open up at the meetings. She had learned to control her drinking problem with Elsie's encouragement and a lot of hard physical labor.

She looked around for something to do. The obvious solution was in front of her. It was time to get her own house in order. She began tearing out the stained and broken kitchen tile. She'd planned on replacing the tile ever since she had bought the house but had kept putting it off. The new tile was sitting in the garage where she had placed it over a year ago.

The air conditioner's motor froze up again, but Jo ignored it and threw open the windows, settling for the slight breeze they offered.

She worked through the night and late into the morning removing the tile and scraping the floor. She spent an hour hauling out the mess and the remainder of the day putting in the new flooring. It was after nine when she wiped away the last of the excess grout. She dropped to the floor in the living room, too exhausted to appreciate her handiwork.

The phone jarred her awake several hours later, she had fallen asleep sitting against the wall. No breeze was stirring, and the house was stifling hot. The streak of sunlight across the living room floor told her it was already afternoon. The phone continued to ring, and she rose slowly to answer it. Her stiff joints ached as she moved.

"Hello." She fell heavily into a chair by the kitchen table and tried to rub the stiffness from her neck.

"Jo? It's Beth. I . . . I was worried about you. When you didn't come back yesterday evening or this morning. I was afraid . . ."

They both remained silent.

"I'm sorry," Beth blurted. "I shouldn't have come on to you like that."

Come on to me, Jo thought, stunned. "It wasn't your fault." They were both speaking at once. Each taking the blame and making lame excuses. Abruptly they both stopped talking. Silence stretched between them.

"Will you come back?" Beth asked softly.

Jo's heart skipped a beat.

"There won't be a repeat of last night," Beth assured her. "I promise."

For some strange reason Jo felt a sharp stab of disappointment in Beth's words. Why? she wondered. Wasn't that what she had wanted? I have to go back, Jo reasoned. She had been contracted to build the room, and it wasn't finished.

"I'll be there before dark. I need to do a few things here first." She thought she heard a sigh from Beth.

"Good. I'll have supper ready."

The hint of intimacy sent a wave of desire through Jo. "Don't bother on my account. I'll eat on the way." She hung up before Beth could reply.


It was almost eleven when Jo's headlights reflected through the cabin windows. Beth had been tossing restlessly in bed for over an hour, unable to sleep. She had expected Jo hours ago. As the time dragged by, so had Beth's doubts.

She was confused about her feelings for Jo. After all, she was supposed to be in love with Janet, who would be returning soon to discuss their future. Why did she want to get involved with a woman who obviously didn't care beans about her? Did Jo find her so completely unattractive? Why had Jo reacted so strongly to a simple kiss? Which, Beth tried to reason, was exactly what it had been. A spur of the moment, didn't-mean-anything kiss.

There was no doubt in Beth's mind that Jo Merrick was a lesbian, so it couldn't be what Beth thought of as the I-know-I-am-but-hope-I'm-not syndrome. She sifted through the conversation she had overhead between Jo and Tracy. Perhaps it was a lover who died, or maybe Jo had just recently broken up. She could even be involved with someone now. At this thought Beth sat up. Why hadn't it occurred to her that Jo might be involved with someone? Because she's so unhappy, she answered without hesitation. The one thing that Jo couldn't hide was the sense of sadness that emanated from her. The only time Beth had seen her smile was over some antic of Tracy's.

It was Jo's behavior with Tracy that had first attracted Beth's attention, well not exactly the *first*, she admitted to herself, recalling Jo's strong hands. Hands that gripped a hammer with firm assurance, and then caressed the baby rabbit with a tenderness that caused Beth to shiver. Beth could still feel the heat that radiated from Jo's hand and how it had trembled at her touch.

Memories of Jo swimming came back to her. Beth's skin tingled as she recalled watching Jo's naked body floating on the gentle swell of the water. She had stood unnoticed for several minutes watching Jo, enjoying the sight. When Jo got out of the water, Beth had deliberately backed up so she could watch the strong sensuous ripple of Jo's muscles as she moved. Jo had walked up to her with such an overpowering sense of assurance and self-possession that it had taken all of Beth's will power not to touch her then.

That's when I fell in love with her. She blinked at the thought and repeated it to herself. It was true. She was in love with Jo. What did that mean to her relationship with Janet?

"It means there shouldn't be one," she admitted aloud. She had never felt this way about Janet. Suddenly a new fear edged its way in and began to eat at her. Did Jo remember who she was? Could that be why she kept pulling away? The San Antonio paper had carried the story of the trial. Had Jo read the articles? Maybe that was why Jo continued to avoid her and had reacted so strongly to the kiss.

And if Jo didn't know, would she condemn her when she found out?

Those thoughts brought with them the haunting specter of telling Tracy. No time would ever be right for telling Tracy the truth about her father. The few times Tracy had brought up the subject of her father, Beth had lied. She had told Tracy that her father was dead.

At the time it seemed easier than telling her the truth, which was that her father was in prison for armed robbery and murder. Plenty of people remembered the trial and its details, and it would be horrible if Beth waited too long and Tracy heard it from someone else. But if she told her too soon and Tracy wasn't able to understand, the consequences could be even more devastating.

This was an almost constant fear now that Tracy was in school. Beth knew she'd have to find a way to tell Tracy soon.

The headlights went out and Jo quietly entered the cabin. Beth slid beneath the sheet when she heard the bolt slide into place and remained still as Jo tiptoed to her own bed and undressed without making a sound. Sleep would be slow in coming.

* * * * *

The smell of coffee woke Beth. She had finally fallen into a troubled sleep just before dawn. She was exhausted from her night of soul searching, but her mind was made up. She loved Jo Merrick and intended to do whatever it took to break through that thick, sad exterior to the smoldering passion that she had glimpsed just below the surface.

# CHAPTER SIX

They spent the day carefully avoiding each other as much as possible. Jo would get Beth started on some project and then go work alone somewhere else. It was after two when Beth decided she was hungry. The outer walls were enclosed and the windows were in.

"I'm going in for a sandwich and some tea. Do you want something?" Beth called.

Jo put down the hammer and wiped her face with her bandanna. "Let me finish this section and I'll be in. It shouldn't take more than five or ten minutes."

"Is tuna salad all right with you?"

"Yeah, that's fine."

Beth went to wash her face and hands. The situation with

Jo was getting ridiculous. They had to work this out. Drying her face, she made up her mind to talk to Jo tonight. They were both adults and should be able to discuss their feelings in an adult manner. She went into the kitchen and pulled jars of mayonnaise and pickles from the refrigerator. Kneeling in front of the sink she opened the door to get a can of tuna. A terrifying hiss and rattle filled the air. It took her a long heart-stopping second to locate the source. Less than three feet in front her was a rattlesnake, coiled and ready to strike. Its head was pulled close to its body while its tail was held up to allow the rattles to issue their ominous warning.

She knew the slightest movement on her part could trigger its attack. Petrified, she watched the snake's rattles continue dancing their deadly signal. Her eyes adjusted to the dimness inside the cabinet, allowing her to distinguish the dark, diamond-shaped pattern and to see the radar-like tongue darting out, searching for the intruder that had disturbed its sleep.

Could she slam the cabinet door faster than it could strike? She stared into its hypnotic ebony eyes, knowing she'd never be able to move faster than it could.

The nearest hospital was in Grayson, which was nearly sixty miles away. Every horror story she'd ever heard about rattlesnake strikes came rushing back to her.

A scene from a movie of a snake embedding its fangs in a woman's neck and her falling dead raced through her thoughts. It doesn't happen that way, she scolded herself and tried to rein in her runaway imagination. She felt a small glimmer of hope as the snake stopped rattling. Maybe if she stayed still long enough it would simply crawl out the same way it had come in.

The longest three minutes of Beth's life passed as she and the snake continued to stare at each other. The sound of the screen door opening nearly stopped Beth's heart. She was afraid to speak to warn Jo, scared her voice would trigger a strike.

She heard Jo move toward the bathroom, and Beth frantically tried to find a way to communicate her situation without moving or making a sound. Jo's footsteps stopped at the bedroom door.

"Are you all right?"

Beth attempted to speak but her throat was constricted with fear. Jo started toward her.

"Stop," Beth whispered, mesmerized by the snake's darting tongue.

"What's wrong?" Jo took another step closer.

Beth watched in horror as the rattles came up and the ominous sound began again. She heard Jo's sharp intake of breath and sensed she had stopped somewhere behind her.

The only sound in the room was the deadly rattles. Burning rivulets of sweat rolled into Beth's eyes, but she didn't dare to even blink them away. She could smell her own fear.

When the snake's deadly warning grew silent, Jo asked in a voice little more than a whisper. "Can you see it?"

Beth was too afraid to speak. When she didn't respond, Jo continued. "Move one finger for yes and two for no." Beth eased up one finger of the hand clutching the door handle.

"Can you move?"

Two fingers.

"I'm going to slowly move toward you."

Beth raised two fingers so quickly that her arm jerked and the rattle began again. They both froze until the snake settled down.

"You're going to have to trust me" Jo said. "Now release the door. Don't move your hand. Just relax your grip."

With slow deliberation Beth raised two fingers.

"Beth," Jo's voice took on a silkiness that caused Beth's breath to catch. She wanted to listen to her but was too scared. "Beth . . . Beth listen to me. Are you listening?

Beth raised one finger.

"Good. I know you're scared and I understand, but you

can't stay like that. You don't know what might set it off. Now please, release the door."

Beth couldn't make herself let go of the handle.

"Think of Tracy. What would she do without you?"

Beth eyed the snake. She wasn't sure she could let go of the handle. Her hand felt welded to it. What was Jo going to do? Suddenly it didn't matter, because she knew Jo wouldn't do anything to endanger her.

"You've got to trust me," Jo whispered. "Relax your hand."

Beth slowly eased her grip on the handle. Without warning, Jo's foot slapped the door from Beth's hand. In the same instant, Beth was in Jo's arms being carried outside where she was overcome by convulsive shakes and tears.

"It's all right." Jo sat on the porch holding Beth and rocking her. "You're safe now."

Beth gave herself over to the sound of Jo's voice and the slow swaying of her body. Jo's arms provided a safe haven for her to rest, and she melted into them.

Her tears faded and the shaking subsided, and she gradually became aware of Jo's hand stroking her hair. Beth unwound her hands and slid them around Jo's neck. Jo stopped rocking and pulled back to gaze at her. With gentle but insistent pressure, Beth pulled Jo's head down to hers. Beth's breath caught when her lips met Jo's and Jo responded. As the kiss grew more urgent, Jo's arms tightened, pulling her closer.

Beth's hand wound into the short, thick, auburn hair that she had been dreaming of. She gasped as Jo's tongue parted her lips and began a subtle dance. Jo's hand caressed her side, each movement drawing closer to the aching nipple that begged for her touch. Beth's head spun in anticipation when, in one smooth move, Jo was on her feet carrying Beth into the house. At the thought of entering the house again, Beth froze.

Jo stopped. "It's all right," she whispered, kissing Beth's

cheek. "If it bothers you, we can stay out here, but you know the snake has left by now."

Beth knew Jo was probably right, but she was still scared.

Jo set her down. "Wait here." She disappeared inside the cabin only to reappear a moment later with a quilt. She took Beth's hand and led her toward the river.

Beth's heart hammered as she watched Jo spread the quilt under a tree. Her mouth grew dry when Jo stripped out of her clothes and moved to her.

Beth began to unbutton her own shirt, but Jo stopped her. With a slight smile Jo finished the job for Beth. With each released button came a feather-light caress before Jo moved to the next button. Beth's legs began to tremble again. She tried to pull Jo closer, but Jo shook her head.

"Wait," Jo murmured, stepping behind Beth and unbraiding her long hair. The aching between Beth's thighs became almost unbearable as Jo combed her fingers through the long strands. Beth turned, and Jo's fingers grasped the button holding Beth's shorts, the back of her fingers brushing against Beth's stomach. Jo knelt before Beth and pulled the shorts down, allowing her fingers to travel the length of Beth's legs. Beth grasped Jo's shoulders for support as Jo's lips brushed across her lower stomach and moved down to nuzzle between her thighs. With gentle firmness Jo removed Beth's hands and held them as her tongue made a trail back up Beth's body. Still holding Beth's hands, Jo kissed her deeply before leading her into the river. The cool water lapped against Beth's hot body, but not even the river could extinguish the burning desire that Jo had kindled.

Jo pulled Beth tightly against her, and Beth closed her eyes, surrendering to the bold hands that roamed her back and the eager mouth that claimed her own.

Beth's toes dug into the soft river bottom as the cool water surged around them. Her hands closed around Jo's breasts and caressed the taut nipples. Jo moaned, but removed Beth's hands and trailed her lips along Beth's jaw, her tongue blazing a path along her neck and around her ear. Beth cried out with pleasure as Jo captured a nipple gently between her teeth, and held it while her tongue flicked rapidly across it. Her hand pressed between Beth's thighs.

"I can't stand up," Beth gasped as Jo's fingers slid inside her.

"Put your arms around my neck," Jo mumbled, without removing her teeth from Beth's nipple.

Beth did as she was instructed. Jo's free arm encircled Beth's waist while her other hand continued to manipulate Beth's burning center. Beth felt the pressure building and wrapped her legs around Jo as the water about them splashed wildly with their violent thrusting. As the orgasm washed over her, Beth buried her face in Jo's shoulder and screamed her pleasure.

Clinging to Beth, Jo waded toward the bank. When they reached the edge of the water, Beth reluctantly released her grip on Jo and waded out. They lay on the quilt without speaking. Beth turned to find a silent Jo staring morosely at the sky, and knew without asking that Jo was already regretting her actions.

# CHAPTER SEVEN

Jo forced herself not to reach for Beth again. She had no right. She belonged to someone else. She had promised to love Diane forever.

Deep down she knew Diane wouldn't have expected her to remain alone, so there really wasn't any reason why she shouldn't be free to love Beth. But if that were true, why did she feel so guilty? Was it because Beth was the first? No one had even vaguely caught her attention in the two years since Diane's death. Or was it because she was alive to feel and enjoy life and Diane wasn't?

"Is there someone else?" Beth's voice cut through Jo's self-flagellation.

How did she answer that? Yes, but she's dead. Or, no, only a ghost.

Beth raised herself up on her elbow. "Talk to me, Jo. After what just happened between us I think I deserve an explanation for why you're suddenly withdrawing."

Jo turned her head to look at Beth. The pain and confusion showed in Beth's eyes. She deserves that much, her conscience prodded.

"There is. Or was," Jo corrected.

Beth waited patiently, trying not to let her fear of losing Jo control her.

"She died two years ago."

Beth reached for Jo's hand. "I'm sorry." She knew there was nothing she could say to ease Jo's pain.

Jo shrugged and stared at the sky.

"Tell me about her," Beth prompted.

Jo hesitated. She had never talked about Diane to anyone except Elsie. She turned to find Beth's gentle gaze upon her and suddenly it felt right to tell her.

"We met at a Christmas party some mutual friends were giving. And from the beginning everything fell into place. We talked for hours at the party and went to her apartment afterward for coffee. We talked until sunrise. There were so many things we had in common. We started dating, and a year later we moved in together.

"My dad had retired a few months before, and he and Mom had moved to St. Louis. I had taken over the business and had a lot of new ideas that eventually increased its net worth. Everything was going great."

She stopped and plucked a blade of grass, shredding it as she continued.

"We had eight wonderful years together. The last year started off so perfect. Diane's business was booming. She was an interior designer and had gone out on her own about three years after we met. She was getting more referrals than she could handle. She had hired a couple of assistants and was thinking about opening another location in Austin."

She sat up, plucked another blade of grass, and continued the shredding ritual. "Merrick Construction had doubled in size. I had hired another crew. Diane and I had started clearing the land for what was supposed to be the beginning of our dream home when she began getting these headaches.

At first we thought it was just stress or allergies, but they kept getting worse and more frequent. She finally saw a doctor. We were putting up the house frame when the doctor called." The pain and fear of the diagnosis came back to Jo. Her breathing became ragged, and tears burned her throat.

Beth's hand rested on her arm. "Don't do this if it's too painful."

Jo shook her head. She wanted, needed, to tell Beth.

"She had beautiful black hair." She recalled how silky Diane's hair felt sliding between her fingers or over her body. She shook her head to chase away the memory.

"It all fell out during the treatments. The pain was unbearable and the treatments made her ill. She was in so much pain during the final stage, and there was nothing I could do. I was such a damn coward I couldn't do the one thing she wanted above all else." Jo stopped and Beth waited in silence, not pushing Jo.

"In the end, all I could do was promise to love her forever." She turned tear-filled eyes to Beth. "I promised to love her forever," she repeated.

Beth sat quietly.

"I'm betraying her."

"Did Diane love you?" Beth asked softly.

"Of course, she did," Jo sputtered, amazed that Beth would ask her such a question.

"Then why would she want you to spend the rest of your life alone and sad?"

"She wouldn't," Jo replied, offended by Beth's suggestion.

"Her last words were that she loved me and for me to be happy."

Beth arched her eyebrows slightly and gave a small smile. "So why are you doing something she wouldn't want?"

Jo sat silently for a long stretch before sighing deeply. "I feel guilty. She was so vibrant and full of life." She ripped up a handful of grass and threw it. "It's not fair that she died so young. She had too many unfulfilled dreams."

"Jo, you can't hold yourself responsible for Diane's death. It sounds as though she had a full, happy life. You can't go on acting like you died the day she did. I'm sure you did everything in your power to make her happy."

"But I didn't." Jo jumped up, but Beth grabbed her before she could leave.

"Jo, it's time to stop running."

Jo leaned into her and began to cry. Beth held her until she had cried herself out. Jo sat up and used her bandanna to dry her eyes and blow her nose. Beth waited until Jo had calmed down before she spoke.

"I can understand your pain. I know I can't imagine the depth of it," Beth said, "and I don't want to sound callous, but you can't allow it to destroy the rest of your life. It's been two years. You're a wonderful person, and you deserve to have happiness and love in your life. Even if you don't think it should be with me." She brushed her hair from her face.

Jo felt the old anger beginning to surface. What right did Beth or anyone else have to tell her how long she should grieve? Beth knew nothing about her love for Diane. "Look, I've had all the lectures. I know my decision probably isn't rational to anyone else, but that doesn't change the way I'm feeling." Jo started to stand, but Beth again put out her hand and stopped her.

"Please, don't leave. I'm sorry." She removed her hand and began to pick at a broken string on the quilt. "I just don't want to see you sacrifice your life to guilt."

"What do you know about guilt?" Jo demanded. She saw Beth flinch at the bitterness of her words.

"Six years ago my father died," Beth began. "My mom left when I was twelve. Dad raised Karen, my older sister, and me. He and I had a special relationship. We were always close." Her voice dropped to a murmur. "Or were until just before he died." She turned her gaze out over the river, and it was Jo's turn to watched as Beth fought to recall her own painful memories.

"I'd met Mark, my ex-husband, a few weeks before Dad died." She struggled to find a way to decide what had happened in those few painful weeks. "I can't explain Mark, even to myself. I didn't love him, but he was so totally different from anyone I'd ever known. He was reckless, didn't care what anyone thought of him, and was completely irresponsible. I was drawn to him like the proverbial moth to a flame."

A hawk screamed overhead. After several seconds Beth drew a ragged breath before continuing. "At first I had no thoughts of becoming involved in a sexual relationship with Mark. I already knew I was a lesbian, and I suspect my father did too. The minute I mentioned Mark, Dad started a personal crusade to get us together. He began badgering me to invite Mark to the ranch for dinner, but I kept refusing. They were such complete opposites. I knew they wouldn't get along." She stretched out on her back and stared at the sky.

"Growing up I was basically the daughter parents dream of. I did good in school and, unlike Karen, I never caused any trouble. I dated the right boys, went off to college, made good grades. Of course, it was in college where I started to slip." She gave a short laugh before continuing. "That was where I began to realize why I preferred being with the girls more than the boys."

Jo stretched out beside her but remained silent.

"Anyway, I let Dad's pressure and Mark's uniqueness convince me that maybe I'd made a mistake about my sexuality, and I started sleeping with Mark. At the time, I thought of it as an experiment. My basic logic was that if I liked being with Mark then I obviously wasn't a lesbian. If I found I didn't like being with him, then I would have to accept the fact that I was a lesbian and live with it." She gave a small, bitter laugh.

"I was so stupid. I didn't know anything about how life really was." She rubbed the bridge of her nose. "To make a long story short, I got pregnant right away. I felt I had no choice but to try for a life with Mark. I decided to introduce him to Dad, and just as I had suspected they hated each other instantly. To make matters worse, Dad was devastated when he found out I was pregnant."

Beth shivered, and Jo pulled the quilt up around her, even though it was much too warm for it. "Mark wanted to get married, but I still had some reservations. He kept pressuring me and eventually I gave in. I thought marrying Mark would make things better, but Dad went through the roof when I told him we were getting married. He got mad and then I got mad. Things went from bad to worse, and I let Mark talk me into eloping. On the way home Mark began to talk about Dad's money. The more he talked the more obsessed he became over the money he was certain Dad had. It didn't take me long to realize why he'd married me." She gave a dry, humorless laugh. "Mark had assumed that because Dad owned three hundred acres he was rich."

Jo rubbed her forehead and said, "Mark obviously wasn't from around here, or he'd have known most ranchers have all of their capital tied up in their land and livestock."

Beth shook her head. "No. He didn't know that Dad was

deeply in debt, that three consecutive years of drought had nearly wiped us out." She fell silent, but Jo perceived she was struggling to tell her more.

"Mark needed money," Beth continued. "Not for any one particular thing. He just craved it, like some people do drugs or alcohol. Sorry."

"It's all right," Jo replied.

Beth's voice dropped to a harsh whisper. "I discovered that I knew nothing about the man I'd married. When we got back and I told Dad we had eloped, he threw me out. Said he wouldn't have trash like Mark living under his roof." Tears ran down her cheek, and Jo restrained the urge to wipe them away, sensing Beth needed to tell her everything. She held Beth's hand.

"Mark was unemployed. All we had to live on was the four hundred dollars that I had in my savings account."

Her voice grew hoarse. "After I finally convinced Mark that Dad didn't have money to give us, he decided we should move to California. He said he had family there who would help us." She ran her hands over her face.

"I didn't want to move, but I thought that being away from Dad for a while would give us both a chance to think about the nasty things we'd said to each other. And I think that deep down I wanted to punish him for not standing by me. I was so angry with him. I wanted to hurt him the way he had hurt me." She sniffed, and Jo offered her already damp bandanna.

"We were in Arizona when Mark stopped at a small isolated grocery store. He said he was going to talk to the owner and see if he'd let him work for a few days. I tried to argue with him because we still had over two hundred dollars from my savings. I told him we should get to California as soon as possible so we could both start looking for work. But he snapped at me and told me to stay in the car."

Jo felt her heart beating faster as Elsie's questions about Beth came back to her. Vague memories began to return.

Fragments from the trial surfaced. The San Antonio paper had made a big production of the good-girl-gone-bad aspect. She reached for Beth's hand again and squeezed. It felt cold despite the afternoon's heat.

"You know, don't you?" Beth asked in a strangled voice.

"I don't remember many of the details. I'd forgotten about it until now."

"Do you want to know the rest?"

"If you want to tell me."

Beth nodded before continuing. "I heard two gunshots. I got out of the car and started running toward the store. Mark came out. He had a gun in one hand and a paper bag in the other. He screamed at me to get back in the car, but I couldn't move. He slapped me and shoved me to the car. Somehow I managed to get back inside the vehicle.

"When I looked up a young girl was running out of the store. She couldn't have been more than twelve or thirteen, and there was blood all over her blouse. When I saw her I thought he had shot her. I tried to get out of the car to help her, but he kept hitting me and dragging me back inside. The girl started screaming at us, and Mark raised the pistol. He was going to shoot her." Beth's voice still held a trace of shock. Jo pulled her trembling body into her arms and held her close.

"You don't have to tell me."

"Yes, I do!"

"All right, but take your time." Beth's breath was labored. "Breathe deep," Jo said, rubbing her back. "We have plenty of time. Slow down."

Gradually Beth's breathing slowed. "I knocked the pistol out of his hand and managed to get the car door open. He sped off, and I fell out of the car. The girl was so distraught that she attacked me. I finally got away from her and ran into the store. A woman lay just inside the door, and a man was lying across the counter. There was so much blood.

"I was scared and ran. I don't know why. I just ran. All I could think of was getting home to Dad. If I could just get home he would make the nightmare go away, like he had when I was little and I had a bad dream." She wiped her eyes with the heel of her hand.

"A patrol car picked me up a little while later. I was walking down the road." She took a deep breath.

"I found out later that Mark had killed the girl's parents and stolen eighty-six dollars. The authorities wouldn't believe me when I told them I didn't know what he had intended to do. My running away didn't help.

"I told them everything I knew, and they arrested Mark three days later. He'd actually gone on to California and was staying with his sister. He didn't think I would tell them where he was going." Beth's hand wrapped around Jo's.

"The girl eventually calmed down enough that she was able to tell the police that she had been in the back of the store when Mark went in. She saw him shoot her parents. She told the police about seeing me fighting to get away from Mark.

"Her testimony, along with the bruises that Mark had left on me, finally convinced them that I was telling the truth. The court took into consideration the fact that I'd never been in trouble before and that I was willing to testify against Mark, and charges against me were dropped." She pulled away from Jo and sat up.

"Dad came to Arizona to be with me during all of this, but things had changed. There was a barrier between us that had never been there before." She shook her head "I was so shocked when I first saw him. I almost didn't recognize him. In that short time he had gotten so old. His hair had gone completely gray, and his shoulders were bent."

Beth shook off the memories. After several seconds she began again. "I know he knew I was innocent, but I'm not sure he ever forgave me for letting myself become involved with Mark. But I never got to tell him how sorry I was. Dad had a heart attack and died two days after we got home. Mark was sentenced to life in prison in Arizona, and I was alone with a three-hundred-acre ranch to run and pregnant."

She looked at Jo. "I decided everything was my fault. If I hadn't gotten involved with Mark, none of those things would have ever happened. Dad would still be alive. I even blamed myself because Mark murdered those people." Jo started to speak, but Beth raised her hand. "I know better now, but it took me a long time to figure that out. It was killing me. I finally realized that I had to let it go or it would destroy me."

Beth took Jo's hand and pulled her up beside her. "I know I'm asking a lot, but you've got to let go of your guilt about continuing to live and enjoying life. Your pain won't bring Diane back. Hold on to her memory and cherish the love you shared. Nothing can ever take that from you, but don't let her death destroy the rest of your life."

A deluge of emotions pounded Jo's body. She wanted to run away, tear down the room — the entire cabin, so she could pound each and every nail again — but Beth's hands were holding hers and the need to feel them was greater than her need to run.

"I'm falling in love with you," she blurted with a sob. "And it scares me. I don't ever again want to go through the pain of losing someone I love."

Beth pulled Jo's head to her breast and cradled her until the sobs stopped. "I love you too," she said, kissing Jo's head. "Jo, if you let the fear of loss keep you from loving, you've already lost. What kind of life will you have if you never allow yourself to love again? No one knows what tomorrow will bring, but one thing is certain: If you don't take the chance at happiness when it comes along, you'll never know what might have been." She could see the uncertainty in Jo's eyes.

"Jo, as horrible as my time with Mark was, I have Tracy. She's a rainbow created from all that horror. And what you feel here," she tapped the area over Jo's heart, "is the rainbow Diane left you. That feeling will be there forever. Nothing can take that away."

She could see the struggle going on in Jo, but there was still one major hurdle Jo had to overcome. Beth took a deep breath. "I'd like to make love to you."

Jo sat silent for several seconds before whispering. "The final break."

"It's not a break, Jo. It's moving on with your life. I'm not asking you to forget her," Beth assured her. "I'm just asking you to let me love you in my own way."

Jo saw the sincerity in Beth's eyes. "Deep down I know you're right," she answered softly, "but I can't let go of that much at once. I'm really trying."

Beth hid her pain. "I believe you," she said after a slight pause. "I'll wait until you're ready. Can I hold you?"

Together they lay back on the quilt. The emotional turmoil of the afternoon soon lulled them to sleep.


When Beth woke it was almost dark, and Jo was nowhere in sight. With a sickening sense of dread she yanked on her clothes, gathered up the quilt, and headed up to the cabin. She hadn't realized she had been holding her breath until she raced around the corner and saw Jo's truck. She hadn't left.

Jo was carrying an armload of bedclothes back into the cabin. When Jo saw her she gave a self-conscious smile.

"I decided I'd better give everything a good shaking to be sure our slithering friend had left the premises."

Beth's legs begin to tremble as she stared through the opened doorway at the cabinet. Jo followed her gaze.

"I took everything out. There was a hole in the back of the cabinet. I think that's probably where it came in. I found some steel wool in my truck, stuffed it in the hole, and covered it with a wooden patch. That should take care of it, but we need to be careful. I don't know where it crawled in from outside, so it's possible it'll show up somewhere else."

A violent chill ran down Beth's spine. Jo dumped the linens on the porch and walked back to her. Beth noticed Jo's slight hesitation before reaching for her. "We'll be extra careful," she said and pulled Beth's head to her shoulder.

"It could've been Tracy who opened that door." Beth shuddered.

Jo was silent for a moment. "I'll drive into town tomorrow and buy some foam sealant. It won't take us long to spray around the underside of the cabin. The foam will expand and fill in any holes under the siding."

Beth slowly relaxed in the safety of Jo's arms. She knew there was nothing they could do but be careful.

"Are you going to be all right sleeping in there tonight?" Jo asked.

"As long as nothing rattles," Beth said, trying to laugh it off, but her earlier scare was still very much with her.

"I need to make the beds. Can you start dinner?"

Beth eyed the cabinet with trepidation.

"Tell me what you want and I'll get it out," Jo offered.

"No. I have to open it some time, so I may as well start now."

"You're sure?"

"Yeah, I'll be fine. Go make the beds." Beth began to speculate what their sleeping arrangements would be.


After eating supper they sat outside and talked of things they liked and disliked, careful to steer away from any conversation that dealt with Mark or Diane.

"Tell me about your family," Beth prompted.

"As I said earlier, my parents moved to St. Louis after my

father retired. He had his own construction company that he built up from a one-man operation. He taught me everything I know about carpentry."

"What about brothers or sisters?" Beth asked when Jo fell silent.

"I'm an only child."

"Wasn't that lonely?"

"Not really. Mom would baby-sit for extra money, so there were always other kids around. I had a wonderful childhood and have always been close to both my parents."

"Are you out to them?"

Jo ran her hands through her hair. There was a long pause before she answered. "No. I've tried to tell them twice, but I always chicken out." She shook her head. " I don't know why I can't tell them. It's really strange because one minute I'm certain they know and the next minute they say or do something to convince me they're totally in the dark."

"Do you think you'll ever tell them?"

"No. Not now. It's too late."

"Why? It's never too late."

Jo sipped her tea and began to tell Beth about Diane wanting a commitment ceremony. "It was the one thing she asked for that I couldn't give her. I know it sounds like it should have been simple, but I couldn't do it."

"Are you ashamed of being a lesbian?"

"Diane asked me the same thing and, no, I don't think I am. I don't really hide my lifestyle anywhere else. It's just my parents." Jo shook her head. "But it's easy to say that I'm out everywhere else when I'm self-employed and don't really have to confront the issue anywhere else in my life except with my parents."

Silence fell between them. "I'm tired of talking about myself," Jo began. "Tell me something about you. You said earlier that your mom left when you were twelve. What happened?"

"I'll let you off the hook this time, but don't think for one minute I don't know what you're doing by changing the subject." Before Jo could argue, Beth moved on.

"Mom got bored with ranch life. She ran off with a local lawyer." Beth leaned forward and stretched her back muscles. "Mom was born and raised in Dallas. She met Dad while he was up there for a cattleman's convention. I don't think she realized how hard it would be living on a ranch. She certainly wasn't prepared for the isolation and the never-ending work. She liked living in Dallas where something was always happening."

"Do you ever see her?"

"Not anymore. She came down for Karen's high-school graduation, but by then she and the lawyer had gotten married and it was too awkward. Plus, it was pretty clear she didn't want us in her life anymore."

"It must have been rough on all of you."

"I think it was worse for Karen. Mom and I never got along very well. I was too much like Dad." Beth shifted in her chair. "I missed her and everything, but Karen took it personally. She always felt like it was her fault that Mom left. She still does, I think."

"What about your dad?"

"I think he was more relieved than hurt. They'd both known for years that they'd made a mistake, and they wasted fourteen years of their lives paying for it."

"You don't sound bitter. I think most people would be."

"Believe me, at first I resented Mom leaving, but after a while I realized that their constant fighting and the anger between them had gotten so bad it was like we'd been granted a reprieve after she left."

"How do you and Karen get along?" Jo asked. "Being an only child, I'm always curious about how siblings interact."

"We were probably about the same as any other sisters. When we were younger we fought a lot. There's two years difference in our ages. She was always interested in makeup and boys, and I liked working the ranch with Dad. As we got older we had more in common. Now her life pretty much revolves around her kids and her husband, and mine around Tracy and the ranch."

"What about Janet?" Jo asked, unable to be silent about Janet any longer.

"Oh," Beth chuckled. "That's a loose end that's not going to be fun tying up." Beth told Jo how she had met Janet.

"Are you in love with her?" Jo asked.

"No. I'm in love with you," Beth answered honestly. "I was in lust with Janet. I had been alone for six years, and she came along at the right time. We've never talked about a lasting relationship. Besides, there are some major points of friction between Tracy and Janet."

Jo felt a spark of joy at this news. She didn't want Beth to be involved with anyone. Jo didn't want Beth to have a chance to swing the conversation back on Jo, so she asked another question.

"When did you know you were gay?"

Beth shook her finger at Jo. "You're very good at controlling a conversation. But to answer your question, in college. I played on the tennis team and had a lot of trouble with my shoulders. My roommate gave great back rubs. One night the massage got really good and . . . well, let's just say I've been a changed woman ever since." Beth began to rebraid her hair.

Jo felt herself growing excited just watching her.

Beth looked up and found Jo's gaze on her, and Jo knew she had been caught.

"What about you?" Beth asked to break the tension.

"The second grade."

"Get outta here."

Jo shook her head. "No. I was in the second grade. Her name was Katie Bass, and she was four months older than me. Her father was a doctor, and she knew all about where babies came from." Jo picked up a twig and began to break it into small pieces. "One day after school we were in my room playing and she proceeded to show me a slightly altered version of how that biological wonder occurred. I knew then and there."

"You've never been with a man?"

"No. But I don't have to drop a brick on my toe to know I wouldn't like it."

Jo was exhausted and she was sure Beth was also, but neither made any mention of going to bed.

Silence sat heavily between them. Finally Jo cleared her throat in a nervous cough and stood. "I guess it's about time for me to turn in."

Beth tried not to seem too anxious as she stood and followed Jo inside. Her heart pounded a heavy staccato when she walked into the bedroom and found the twin beds pushed together.

"I hope I wasn't being presumptuous," Jo said, folding her arms in a self-conscious gesture across her chest.

"No. It's fine." Beth felt like a bumbling teenager again. She wanted this woman more than she had ever wanted anyone, and she knew that if she moved too fast she'd lose her. *If Jo can't reconcile her guilt about Diane's death, I'll lose her anyway.* To hide her desire and nervousness, Beth grabbed her gown and headed to the bathroom for a cold shower.

The cabin was dark when she emerged. Her eyes adjusted to the darkness as she crossed the room. She was surprised to see Jo sitting on the side of the bed. Beth sat next to her and waited for her to speak.

"I didn't know which side of the bed you wanted," Jo murmured.

"It doesn't matter," Beth replied, reaching for Jo's hand. Jo jumped at her touch, and Beth's heart went out to her. "It's all right. We don't have to do anything."

"I feel like a fool," Jo blurted. Beth could hear the confusion in her voice.

"Jo, I understand how hard this is for you. I love you and

101

I'm willing to wait as long as it takes. I want more from you than just sex."

"I'm trying, but . . ."

Silence fell between them. Beth leaned over and kissed Jo's cheek, which sent a jolt through her body. I'll wait until she comes to me, she admonished herself.

"I'll wait," she promised.

# CHAPTER EIGHT

Jo stood on the porch holding a cold cup of coffee and watching a small herd of deer that had wandered down from the hills. She felt emotionally raw and exhausted. Her feelings were bouncing around like a Ping-Pong ball. One minute she wanted to scream her happiness in finding Beth, and the next she was riddled with guilt for betraying Diane's memory. Perhaps it has nothing to do with Diane at all, a tiny voice nagged. Maybe you're just afraid of letting yourself feel anything for anyone again.

Disgusted with the never-ending circle of confusion, she tossed out the contents of the cup and went back inside. Beth was sitting on the couch reading a paperback.

"I'm going to Dodson to get the sealant," Jo said. "Do you want anything?" She needed to be alone now, and going into town was a perfect excuse to get away. She waited, worried that Beth might want to go with her.

"No. I brought a book with me. Since I can't do anything without you here, I'm going to spend the day being lazy."

Jo made a hasty, if somewhat obvious, escape. She drove slowly down the dirt road and across an old rickety wooden bridge with high iron railings on either side. Jo held her breath, determined not to think about the stability of the bridge or the screeching protest it made as she crossed. She turned the radio on in an attempt to drown out the bridge noises and the incessant rattling of her old truck.

The weather bureau was predicting rain. Jo gazed hopefully at the clear sky, knowing that neither the sky nor the weather bureau meant much. Either or both could prove wrong. If there was any predictability about Texas weather, it was that it's unpredictable. If it did start to rain, she'd have to hurry back or chance not being able to get in over the poorly maintained road.

Her thoughts strayed to Beth, causing her to begin a gentle probe of her feelings. Was she in love with Beth? Yes. The answer came quickly with no reservations. "So why do I feel like shit?" she asked herself aloud. Was she ready for another relationship? No! Yes. Maybe. "I don't know," she admitted, running her fingers through her windblown hair. What about her promises to Diane? Did they dissolve simply because Diane had died? Her thoughts raced back and forth until, somewhat startled, she realized she was already in the small town of Dodson. She pushed away her pondering to concentrate on her driving.

At the hardware store she found the sealant. Still no closer to a decision on what she should do about her feelings for Beth, she bought a cold soft drink at a convenience store and drank it as she drove to the city park. A few people were at picnic tables eating lunch. Jo found a quiet, shady spot, sat on the ground, and rested her back against a tree. A gentle breeze stirred her hair. Determined to reach a decision, she stretched her legs before her and made up her mind to settle this thing. She couldn't continue with this indecision. It wasn't fair to Beth, and it wasn't fair to her. Before she got back to the cabin today she was determined to come to some kind of decision.

"Hi."

Startled, Jo opened her eyes to find a young, blue-eyed boy standing next to her. He couldn't have been more than three. He was clutching a small, tattered teddy bear.

"You sleepin'?" he asked, staring at her with open curiosity.

She eased into a more comfortable position. "Yeah, I guess I was."

"What's your name?"

"Jo. What's yours?"

"Andy."

"Who's your friend?" She tugged the bear he clutched.

"Dimples. Mommy Penny named him that 'cause he's got dimples like me."

"Let me see."

He held up the bear. There were bright red patches beside its mouth.

"Let me see your dimples."

He gave her such a large smile that Jo found herself laughing.

"Andy!" A young woman with spiked black hair, who was several months pregnant ran to them. "I'm sorry," she panted. "He was playing in the sandbox and I just turned around for a minute and he was gone."

"He's been introducing me to Dimples," Jo said, standing up and brushing off the seat of her shorts. The woman took Andy's hand.

"I hope he didn't bother you," she added as she brushed back his curly blond hair.

"No. We were just enjoying the day," Jo said and started to leave.

"Can you build a road?" Andy demanded.

Jo stopped and looked down at him. He was staring at her with great sincerity. She knelt down in front of him. "I'm a carpenter. I build houses."

"But can you build a road?" he persisted.

"Andy," the woman cut in. "Leave her alone." She turned to Jo. "He's a little upset with me. I can't sit on the ground and help him build his road." She patted her abdomen.

"I see," Jo answered, standing up.

Andy was watching Jo closely and apparently saw a potential road builder.

"Can she eat with us?" Andy asked, tugging at the woman's arm.

Both women stood caught in the uncomfortable moment.

"Can she?" he demanded again.

"Sure. If she'd like." She looked at Jo with clear gray eyes. "There's plenty to eat, if you don't mind serious junk food."

Jo looked at her watch. It was twelve-twenty. "I should be heading back." Jo hesitated. She wasn't ready to go back.

"Why don't you join us?" The woman asked, studying Jo. "You look like you could use a pit roasted hot dog and some fat-filled chips. It's Andy's favorite lunch," she added with an adorning gaze at the child.

"Pleeese," he begged, looking up at Jo.

Jo hesitated a moment too long, and the woman extended her hand. "I'm Reva Mifflin, and I guess you've already met Andy and Dimples."

Jo gave in and shook her hand. "Jo Merrick." She was no closer to a decision and wasn't eager to head back to the cabin.

"Andy's birth mother is a driller and is working off shore this week. So Andy and I decided we needed to give ourselves a long lunch to enjoy a picnic today. Didn't we, sport?" Andy nodded vigorously as they walked.

Jo tried not to stare at the woman as they settled down at

a well-laden picnic table near the playground. Her internal dyke-alert was flashing, but Dodson didn't seem to be the most obvious place to find two lesbians raising a family.

"Help me build a road," Andy insisted.

"Andy, go play," Reva told him. He started to protest until she gave him a look that he apparently knew meant business. He headed off to the sandbox again, while Reva kept up a continuous line of chatter about Andy and the expected baby that was due next month.

"We already know it's going to be a girl," she rushed on. As she talked, Jo felt the muscles in her body relax. "Penny," Reva's dark eyes flickered over Jo, "my lover, has already given her notice. Drilling pays great but she's away from home too much." She dumped a small bag of charcoal into a grill. "I won't be able to handle the store and both kids, so we've decided to try to make it on just the store's revenue alone."

"Store?" Jo asked, munching on a chip.

"Um, yeah," Reva said, holding the can of starter fluid. "Listen, I hate to sound like such a wuss, but this stuff scares the crap out of me. Would you mind?"

"No, not at all." Jo took the can and squirted the liquid over the charcoal. A moment later she dropped in a match and waited for it to burn down. "What kind of store do you have?" Jo prompted.

"An antique shop. Lone Star Antiques. It's here in Dodson. Business has been slow today, so Andy and I are treating ourselves to a long lunch. We usually do a pretty good business. For some reason people from San Antonio love to drive up here looking for antiques. I don't dare tell them how much of our inventory was picked up from estate sales in San Antonio."

Jo chuckled. "That would destroy the sense of country charm, wouldn't it?" She watched until the charcoal had burned down enough to douse it a second time.

"Be careful," Reva called, taking a step farther away from the grill.

Jo stood back and dropped in the match, moving away as the fire emitted a loud whooshing noise.

"I hate it when it does that," Reva said with a shudder.

"How long have you and Penny lived in Dodson?

"Penny was born here. We met five years ago in college and moved here after we graduated. We both wanted to refurbish antique furniture, and the store was a way to support ourselves and give us an outlet to sell the furniture. So it worked out well." She placed hot dogs over the glowing coals. "Plus, we both wanted kids, and this seemed like a decent place to raise them."

Jo wondered at the women's courage to raise a family and be open about their lifestyle in such a small town.

"Don't you get harassed?" she asked.

"Not too much. There are a few assholes, but you get those no matter where you live. It's important to both of us that our kids grow up in a small town. Do you have kids?"

Jo shook her head, but soon found herself telling Reva about Tracy. Over lunch and with Reva's gentle probing, Jo surprised herself by telling her about Diane and about Beth.

"Don't rush it," Reva said, patting Jo's arm. "Time usually takes care of everything. When the time is right, these things have a way of just falling into place."

Jo didn't verbalize her doubts that anything would ever fall into place again.

After lunch Andy returned to the sandbox but soon reappeared with a truck full of sand. He coerced Jo into helping him build his road. As they moved and packed the narrow trail of sand, she found herself thinking of Tracy and wondering what she had been like as a baby. Watching Andy and Reva made her realize she wanted to be back at the cabin with Beth. She wanted to find the happiness that Reva and Penny had found. It was time to move on with her life. She couldn't bring Diane back, but she could hold her forever with the special memories they had made.

Brushing the sand from her hands, Jo thanked Andy and

Reva for lunch and left with a promise to visit their shop the next time she was in town. As she got back onto the highway she noticed that the clouds were building in front of her. It was probably raining at the cabin. Rain in the drought-stricken area would mean new life. "A new beginning," Jo whispered happily.

By the time Jo reached the dirt road leading to the cabin, the rain was so heavy she could barely see. The weather bureau had issued a flash flood warning, and although it wasn't storming here yet, there was a tornado watch in effect until eight that evening. The small ditches and creeks were already running swiftly.

She leaned closer to the windshield in an attempt to see better, trying not to think about Beth and the river. Jo reassured herself that Beth had grown up around the river. She would know if she needed to ride out. But remembering the narrow ledge they had ridden on to get to the cabin that first day made her shudder. Crossing it in this rainstorm would be tricky.

She wondered briefly if she should even try to get to the cabin or if she should go back to town. A glance at the water rushing along the roadside told her she wouldn't be able to turn around. She had no choice but to go forward.

Even at the snail's pace she was traveling the tires lost traction and slipped, forcing her to maneuver it back into the center of the road. She was grateful now that no one else used the road.

She was more than five miles from the cabin when the truck's rear end swung sharply to the left. She steered into the skid to regain control, but the mud was too slippery. The truck continued to slide until it bumped against a tree.

Jo was stuck. She accelerated and cursed as the truck failed to budge. She looked around inside the truck for something to throw over her to keep from being drenched. Rain hadn't been an issue for so long, however, that any umbrella or coat she may have once had in there had long since been taken out. She used her hand to wipe the condensation off the back window. The truck's camper made it too dark to see inside. She made a mental review of the contents in the truck. There was nothing she could use to stuff under the wheels to give them traction.

She had two choices. She could sit here and wait for the rain to stop and hope the flooding didn't reach her, or she could walk to the cabin. The sound of water rushing beneath the truck finalized her decision. She stepped out into water, which was already halfway to her knees. She clung to the truck for as long as she could, then slowly made her way to the middle of the road. The pounding rain plastered her shirt and shorts to her skin; mud sucked at her sneakers, making them heavy and burdensome.

The water on the roadside was rising rapidly, and it would soon be high enough to get into her truck. The water and mud would ruin the motor. The truck wasn't the greatest vehicle, but it was hers and it was paid for. The power tools in the back of the truck would be destroyed as well.

She glanced back over her shoulder, trying to see how far up the sides of the truck the water had risen. Without warning her feet flew from beneath her, and she crashed into the slippery muck.

"Damn." She struggled to stand up. She tried to wash herself off with the falling rain, but the mud just smeared. She took a few more steps and fell again. She focused her attention on maintaining her balance.

When Jo approached the bridge, she stared in horror. The same gentle moving river in which she had made love to Beth just yesterday was now a raging force bent on destruction. The water had risen to just below the bridge floor.

Her heart missed a beat at the thought of having to cross the bridge that had been creaking and heaving even before the high water. Here and there she could see plumes of water shooting up from between the planks of the bridge. If the water kept rising it would soon cover the floor of the bridge.

She considered turning around and walking back to Dodson. The sound of snapping branches caused her to look up. A huge uprooted tree was being carried along by the swirling, muddy mass.

The tree was rushing around the bend in the river, ripping away everything that got in its way. In a matter of seconds it would crash into the old bridge and wipe out her access to Beth.

Without consciously making a decision, Jo started running across the bridge. The water roared beneath her. The boards vibrated with its fury. She kept her eyes focused on the far side, trying not to see or think about the churning demon below her or the rapidly approaching tree.

She was still several feet from the end when the structure gave a sickening shudder. An ear-splitting crash followed as the tree collided with the bridge. The impact of the tree striking the bridge knocked her down, but Jo was up and moving before her body could register the pain. The boards began to fall away behind her. The structure trembled as if some giant hand had grabbed it and shook it about. The old bridge gave a painful shriek as it broke apart.

Jo jumped as far as she could and managed to grab a support beam that had been set in concrete into the bank. She clung to it as the bridge folded inward and tore loose. The savage rain beat down into her face, making it difficult to see.

Beams exploded, sending clouds of dirt and debris into the air. A piece of the debris slapped into her leg. She screamed as the impact knocked her sideways and almost broke her grip. Recovering her hold, she dangled from the mud-slick support and watched as the mangled bridge and tree swept downstream and out of sight.

A large section of the bank broke loose and fell into the swirling mass. Jo realized that the beam she was clinging to could go at any moment. She tried to sink her foot into a toehold, but the pain in her leg prevented her from asserting enough pressure to keep from slipping. She stopped to gather her strength, and with one major effort, she pulled herself up the slope. Just as she did, the beam she had been clinging to started to slide.

Jo scrambled up the muddy bank. She was almost to the top when she slipped and a large section of the bank gave way beneath her. Terrified, she clawed at the bank only to grab handfuls of loose mud. She was sliding downward. Water slapped against her feet. Her hand closed over a small length of root sticking out of the mud, but before it could stop her fall she was waist-deep in water.

The river yanked at her, trying to pull her under. Jo clung to the root, which was no more than an inch in diameter. Her wet muddy hand was slipping down the short length of root. Praying it wouldn't pull loose or break, she struggled to hang on to it and wrap it around her wrist to take the pressure off her dangling body.

The water continued to whip her around. She managed to grab the root with her free hand as well and fought to get her feet under her. Something brushed up against her leg beneath the water. Jo turned in time to see what appeared to be a quilt caught on a large branch. The branch got caught in a large whirlpool and sucked into the swirling mass.

The sight of the branch disappearing into the whirlpool gave her a fresh shot of adrenaline. She gathered her muscles and pulled herself upward, until at last she could feel her feet brush bottom. As she continued to struggle, small chunks of mud began falling away from the area around the base of the root. She held her breath and dug her toes into the muddy bank. With her free hand, she grabbed every possible handhold, until her body finally cleared the water.

Slowly she continued to inch her way up the bank. When she reached the base of the root she was reluctant to release it. The root had become her lifeline. With slow deliberation she unwound the root and carefully pulled herself up until she reached the top of the riverbank.

Wanting to get as far away from the river as possible, she limped several yards down the road before she dropped to her knees. Her body ached and her muscles shook from exertion.

She didn't know how long she knelt there in the rain. As some point she became aware that she was shivering from cold rather than exertion. Her leg throbbed. She moved around to examine the damage. She had been hit hard. A large knot encircled the cut. She massaged the muscle slowly and tried to wipe away the mud and blood that clung to her leg. She wiped at her leg, but she couldn't see how deep the cut was. She gave up and chose not to think about infection.

A bright streak of lightning, followed by a clap of thunder so intense it jarred the ground, made her forget about the cut. She started running as fast as the slippery mire would allow.

It was beginning to get dark by the time the cabin was in sight. She stared in horrified awe at what had been the meadow between the cabin and the river. The meadow was now completely under water. She could see waves rolling up near the back of the cabin, and the river was still rising. She found herself praying that Beth had already left for the safety of the ranch.

A jagged spear of lightning struck somewhere nearby, providing Jo with the final burst of energy she needed to make her way up the hill. She experienced a series of conflicting emotions when the cabin door opened and Beth came running to meet her. Her exhaustion was forgotten as she floundered through the mud. Only one thing mattered now, and that was to let Beth know how much she loved her.

# CHAPTER NINE

Beth slipped to one knee but scrambled up and continued to run. She had been pacing for hours waiting for Jo to return.

During the murder trial she had been scared, but it didn't compare to the depth of her fear for Jo today. She had made a dozen mental journeys over every inch of the treacherous road leading from the cabin to Dodson, and always she came back to the ancient bridge that should have been replaced years ago.

Sick with fear for both Jo's and her safety, she had watched as the water steadily made its way closer and closer to the cabin. She knew the wisest thing for her to do was to get on her horse and ride back to the ranch, but she couldn't leave the cabin. She was certain Jo would try to make it back here rather than remain in Dodson. Beth wasn't sure Jo would remember the winding way overland back to the ranch. Beth had finally made the decision to stay and had turned the horse loose, knowing it would make its way to safety.

As Jo came into sight, Beth's heart lurched when she saw blood all over the front of Jo's shirt and down one of her legs. Beth tried to run faster, only to fall face first into the slippery ooze. Then Jo was picking her up.

Ignoring the rain that streaked through the mud on her face, Beth struggled to regain her footing.

"You're hurt," she babbled as Jo steadied her. Beth had a dozen questions, but they were stopped by Jo's lips greedily devouring her own. It was a deep, hungry, soul-consuming kiss that for a moment drove away the fear, the weather, and the rushing river.

Beth felt Jo's body trembling and held tighter as Jo buried her face in Beth's neck. Jo was mumbling something, but Beth couldn't hear her over the storm.

"Come on." She tugged on Jo's hand, and together they struggled back to the cabin.

Once inside Beth grabbed the old flashlight she had found earlier when the electricity had gone out. The batteries were weak but still had enough power to provide a decent light.

"Where are you hurt?" she demanded, pulling Jo closer to the sparse light offered by the window and shining the flashlight on Jo's bloodstained shirt.

Jo looked down as if surprised to see the blood.

Jo appeared to be in shock. "Where are you hurt?" Beth demanded as the storm pounded against the cabin with the same intensity that Beth's heart was pounding against her chest.

"My leg," Jo answered vaguely, looking down at her left leg and turning it so Beth could see.

Beth knelt and examined Jo's leg in the dim reflection offered by the flashlight. She tried to see how deep the wound was, but there was too much mud and blood to tell.

"I'll have to clean it." She pulled Jo to the kitchen sink. "Can you get up on the counter and put your leg in the sink? I'll have to get the mud off before I can see how bad the cut is."

Jo stared at the sink for several seconds before nodding and struggling to pull herself onto the counter. Beth saw that Jo's arms were trembling from the minor exertion.

"I thought the sight of blood made you faint." She tried to smile to hide her growing fear of their situation.

"Only someone else's," Jo reminded her, as her hand reached out and stroked Beth's hair. "I was afraid I wouldn't make it back to tell you how I felt."

Jo's words and touch sent a jolt of energy through Beth, but she had to turn her attention to Jo's leg. This was not the time to act on amorous feelings. Beth cleaned the wound as gently and thoroughly as possible. It wasn't as bad as it had looked, but there was a large knot and a nasty bruise.

"You could probably use a couple of stitches, but the best I can do is clean it and wrap it in gauze." On the way to the bathroom to retrieve the first-aid kit, Beth glanced out the windows. The river was still rising. She checked the back door and saw that water was beginning to seep in. A loud clap of thunder caused the house to vibrate. She rushed to get the kit.

"Jo," she said, and began taping the gauze into place. "I know you're exhausted, but we're going to have to leave soon. Do you think you can walk back to the ranch?"

Jo nodded her head, but her eyes were closed.

Beth wasn't sure Jo even knew what she was telling her, but she rushed on anyway. "We need to make a decision. The storm is getting worse, so it'll be dangerous going out into it, but water is seeping in the back door." Beth watched as Jo visibly tried to pull herself together.

Jo sat up straighter and swung her legs down. "Can we ride double on your horse?"

"No. I let the horse go over an hour ago. I wanted to be

certain he could make his way out safely." She looked at Jo and cupped her cheek in her hand. "I didn't know when you'd be back."

Jo placed her hand over Beth's. "You should've left. What would you have done if I'd stayed in town to wait out the storm?"

Beth shrugged. "I knew you wouldn't."

Jo shook her head and slid to the floor. She swayed and placed her hand on the counter for support. "How long will it take us to walk back to the ranch?"

Beth's forehead knitted in concentration. "I'm not sure. I've never walked up here. But our biggest problem is the storm. The lightning is so bad it's not safe to be out there."

Jo rubbed her hands over her face. "Are there any places where the water could cut us off from the ranch?"

Beth shook her head. "I don't think so. The river flooded once before when I was a kid and this area was under water, but I don't remember any damage at the ranch. I'm just worried about the lightning." They walked to the bedroom to gaze out the back windows and study the swirling river.

"I guess we'll have to decide what's more dangerous, the storm or the river." Beth said.

"I've seen what the river can do. I'll take my chances with the lightning," Jo said. "I've never seen anything like that tree rushing toward me on that bridge. I don't think you've ever seen the full savage power of this river."

"I don't think I want to wait around and see it," Beth said. "Let's go."

Jo looked around the cabin. "Should we try to carry anything with us? If the water gets much higher it'll be in the cabin."

Beth glanced around her. "No. There's nothing here that can't be replaced. We'll travel as light as possible and hope the storm lets up soon." She snatched up the flashlight.

They stepped off the porch and waded into the now ankle-deep water. As they made their way down the small hill the cabin sat on, the water grew deeper. Beth was beginning to doubt their decision to leave. The water would reach their knees before they climbed out of the small valley. With one last look back at the cabin, they began trudging along the waterlogged trail that led to the ranch.

Beth tried not to think about the lightning that crackled around them or about how exposed they were. She was suddenly reminded of the day she'd left for college. She'd been afraid to fly and her father had laughed, telling her that she had a greater chance of being struck by lightning than dying in a plane crash. Those words were meant to comfort her then, but now they took on an ominous new meaning. When they approached the narrow ledge, Jo hesitated.

"It looks worse than it is," Beth yelled over the rain and storm. "It won't be bad. Just stick close to the wall."

Jo rolled her eyes. "As though I wouldn't anyway. I'll be so close to the damn wall you'll think I'm part of it."

Beth was right. Crossing the ledge was easy, but going downhill on the other side proved to be much more difficult. Jo led the way, and Beth noticed the number of times Jo slipped. She wished they could have taken time for Jo to rest, but the storm wouldn't wait. She wondered where Jo's truck was or how far she'd had to walk in this downpour, but it took too much effort to talk while picking their way through the mud in the dim glow of the flashlight

Beth held her questions and instead dreamed of a hot bath and her bed. Would Jo stay with her? She pushed the thoughts away. Jo would let her know when she was ready. Memories of the kiss they had shared at the cabin came back to her, flooding her with warmth. She let it play over and over in her mind and wasn't aware that Jo had stopped walking until she plowed into her.

Jo's arms encircled her weakly and steadied her. "Are you all right?" she asked, slowly releasing Beth.

"Yeah. I wasn't paying attention where I was going."

"I think the worst of the storm has passed over. I'm sorry

to slow us down, but I have to rest." She was breathing in ragged gasps as the rain continued to pound down on them.

Beth had been so absorbed in her thoughts that she hadn't noticed the storm's passing. The heavy clouds were moving away, allowing the sky's natural glow to light their way. Ashamed that she hadn't been more aware of Jo's fatigue, she mentally kicked herself and began looking around for a place where they could rest without sitting in mud.

"Can you make it up to those rocks?" She pointed to a flat section with several large boulders about a hundred feet up the hillside. Jo looked at them and then at the mud around her and nodded. Beth tried to help, but Jo shook her head and climbed toward the boulders.

The night's darkness was beginning to blanket the landscape, and still the rain continued. They sat with their backs together in an attempt to provide each other some support. Beth was tired, and she knew that Jo was in much worse shape.

"What happened to your truck?"

"I slid into a roadside ditch." Jo's voice was heavy with fatigue as she related the events that had led to her getting to the cabin.

Jo described the bridge being torn away and how she had barely made it across, then fell silent.

Beth sat listening to the sound of rain pounding down on them. Jo was beginning to doze, so, being careful not to disturb her, Beth lifted her arm and squinted at the time. It was too dark to see the hands, and Jo had the flashlight.

They weren't halfway to the ranch yet, but she'd let Jo sleep for twenty minutes before waking her.


Jo's eyes flew open. It was now dark and the rain was only a fine drizzle. She hunched her shoulders, and Beth's head snapped up.

"You awake?" Beth asked softly.

Jo stretched her cramped muscles and rubbed her hands over her face. She grimaced at the mud she could feel caked on her face and hands.

"Yeah. I'm sorry. I didn't mean to fall asleep."

"I was going to wake you after twenty minutes, but I fell asleep too," Beth explained. She took the flashlight from Jo and flicked it on. "We've been sleeping almost an hour," she said, glancing at her watch.

"At least the rain has stopped," Jo said. She moaned and eased her body into a standing position. Her injured leg hurt when she first stepped down, but as she continued to walk around, it became less painful.

"Shall we get started again?" Beth asked.

"We may as well. I'm too tired to mud wrestle." Jo moved slowly. Everything hurt.

Beth gave a tired laugh as she stood and stretched. Taking the light from Jo, she flashed the beam ahead of them. "Think of the tales you can tell your grandchildren."

Jo studied Beth's profile in the dim light. She longed to tell her that she wanted them to share the tale together with their grandchildren, but this didn't seem like the time or place. She would wait and take her somewhere special, someplace where they could talk and wouldn't be covered in mud.

Beth caught her staring. "What's wrong?"

Jo looked at Beth's splattered face and knew her own was as bad or even worse. "You have a little something on your face," she said, and smiled.

At the bewildered look from Beth, Jo laughed out loud. Beth continued to stare, and it was Jo's turn to ask what was wrong.

"That's the first time I've heard you laugh," she said. "I like it."

Jo smiled and shrugged. "I haven't felt like laughing in a long time."

"I hope that changes," Beth said before starting down the rocks. "We need to get back. Ernie will be worried."

Jo's smile faded as Beth set a steady pace down the side of the hill to the trail. She wondered why Beth had been so abrupt. Maybe she was she having second thoughts. Jo was too tired to pursue it now. It could wait until they'd had a hot bath and sleep.

Less than an hour later, they met Ernie and Carl leading Beth's horse. Even in the diffused lighting that came from the large flashlight Carl was carrying, Jo could see Ernie's relief when he stepped down from his horse.

"Are you two okay?" Ernie asked, placing a hand on Beth's shoulder.

Beth gave him a big hug. "Yes, but am I ever glad to see you. Is Tracy okay? Is everything all right at the house?"

"Tracy's fine. She and Wanda were baking cookies the last I heard." He scratched his cheek. "The river would have to rise pretty high to ever reach the ranch. The wind did a little damage. There's some tree limbs down, and a section of the barn roof was ripped loose, but that's about it."

Beth walked over to Carl and took the reins of the extra horse.

Ernie turned to Jo. "How you doing?" he asked.

"Tired, but in one piece," Jo responded.

Beth rode over to Jo. "We can ride double."

"Sorry I didn't bring another horse," Ernie said, as he helped Jo onto the horse. "We thought Beth was at the cabin alone," he explained. "When the horse came in just after dark without Beth, I decided we'd better come looking for her.

"This is fine," Jo assured him. She was so exhausted she didn't even worry about being astride a horse.

"Are you hurt?" Ernie asked, spying the now filthy bandage on her leg.

"It's nothing. I'll be fine as soon as I get a bath and some sleep." She longed to lay her head on Beth's back and rest, but realized she'd probably fall off the horse if she did. She was so tired, she suspected she would never be able to get up if she fell.

Ernie handed Beth a cell phone. "Wanda made me promise to call as soon as we found you. She and Tracy were both worried."

Beth took the phone and squeezed Ernie's hand. "What would I do without you and Wanda?"

"You'd manage," Ernie said, but gave Beth's arm a reassuring pat. They headed back toward the ranch.

Jo listened as Beth talked first to Ernie's wife then to Tracy.

"Hi, sweetie," Beth said. Jo smiled, knowing Tracy was on the other end. "I'm fine," Beth reassured her. "No, we weren't hurt. I let the horse go so Jo and I could walk back." Beth laughed and continued. "Yes, Jo is with me and she's fine also. Yes, she took real good care of me. Okay. Hold on."

Beth passed the phone back to Jo. "Tracy would like to say hi to you."

The phone felt heavy in Jo's hand.

"Hello, Tracy."

"Are you okay, Jo?"

"Yeah. We're a little wet from the rain, but we're fine. How about you?"

"I'm spending the week with Wanda and Ernie. They have a puppy, and I get to play with it."

"That's good. Are you sure Shelly won't be jealous?"

Tracy laughed, and Jo warmed at the sound.

"No." Tracy assured her. "Toys can't get jealous."

"If you say so," Jo said. "I'll see you soon, and you can tell me all about the puppy, okay?" Jo could barely keep her eyes open.

"Okay, 'night Jo."

"Good night Tracy. Here's your mom."

Jo handed the phone back to Beth and dropped her head against Beth's back. She was so tired she didn't care if she did fall off the horse as long as she could sleep.

# CHAPTER TEN

When the ragged group arrived at the ranch, Janet's car was parked in the driveway. Beth saw that the bedroom light was on, and for a brief moment she wished they had stayed at the cabin. The river's fury would seem mild in comparison to Janet's when Beth told her it was over between them. Even if things never progressed with Jo, Beth knew it was time for her to break off the affair with Janet. There had to be more to a relationship than sex.

They walked the horses to the gate that led into the backyard, where the security light cast a bright glow.

"I'll take care of the horses," Carl said. Ernie, Beth, and Jo dismounted. As Carl led the horses away, Beth considered following him. Maybe she could just hide in the barn until Janet left. She knew that she was being foolish and that Jo was about to drop in her tracks.

"Why don't you go on in?" she told Jo. "You can use the room you stayed in before. Take a long hot bath. You should find everything you need already there, and I'll find you something to change into as soon as I come in."

Jo hesitated a moment before nodding. "Thanks for the rescue, Ernie."

"Anytime, Jo."

Beth waited until Jo reached the porch before she turned to Ernie.

"How long has she been here?" she asked, nodding toward Janet's car.

Ernie shrugged. "She wasn't here when we left, and that was around seven-thirty."

Beth chewed her lower lip.

"Time to pay the piper, huh?" Ernie asked.

"Shut up," Beth growled.

Ernie chuckled and started to the barn.

"Hey," Beth called. "Thanks for everything you did tonight, and thank Wanda for watching Tracy."

"No problem. I'm just glad you were both all right. That river is nothing to mess with."

"You would have missed me, wouldn't you?" Beth teased.

"Hell yes," Ernie retorted. "I'm too old to be unemployed." Laughing, he walked into the darkness leaving Beth no option but to go in.

Janet was sitting at Beth's desk. The glow from Janet's laptop screen told Beth she'd been working. Janet looked up and crinkled her nose as Beth walked in.

"My god, what have you been doing? You're covered from head to foot in mud."

Beth was too tired to explain everything that had happened. "I got caught out in the storm."

Janet lowered the lid on her laptop and stood. "Why don't you get out of those wet clothes and I'll run you a hot bath?" She walked into Beth's bathroom to start the water.

Beth rummaged through dresser drawers until she found an old robe that had belonged to her father. Beth's clothes wouldn't fit Jo, so that would do until they could wash and dry Jo's shirt and shorts.

"I'll be back in a minute," Beth called, not wanting Janet to follow her out.

Janet stuck her head out the door. "Where are you going?"

Beth hesitated before walking to the door. "I'll explain when I get back."

Janet walked into the bedroom and eyed the robe Beth was holding. "Is someone else here?"

Beth held up a hand. "Please. Just give me a few minutes and then I'll —" She stopped. She was so tired. All she really wanted to do was sleep. Instead she walked out the door, careful to close it behind her.

Beth took the robe down the hall and knocked on Jo's door. There was a muffled reply from within. Beth found Jo in the tub, submerged to her chin in fluffy suds.

"I'm jealous," Beth said as she placed the robe on a chair near the tub.

"You could join me," Jo ventured.

Despite her exhaustion Beth felt a flame of desire. "I'd like that, but I can't yet. I have to take care of something."

"Will I see you later tonight?"

Beth stared at the floor and tucked her hands into the back pockets of her jeans. "I don't know. I'm not sure how things will go." She started to pick up Jo's clothes. "I'll throw these in the washer for you."

"Don't bother. I know where it is," Jo said. Beth noticed a touch of coolness in Jo's voice.

Beth nodded and gently placed the clothes back on the floor. She turned to leave.

"Beth."

"Yes?"

"Is it Janet? Does the car out front belong to her?"

Surprised, Beth's head came up. She had hoped Jo hadn't noticed the car. She wasn't ready to get into this with Jo. She had to settle things with Janet first. All she could do to answer Jo's question was nod.

Jo nodded in return. After an awkward pause, Beth left, softly closing the door behind her.

Janet was standing in the hallway when Beth came out of Jo's room. Neither of them spoke until they were back in Beth's room with the door closed.

"Who is she?" Janet demanded.

"The carpenter."

"What carpenter?"

"I hired a carpenter from San Antonio to build a room onto the cabin."

Janet's look of confusion reminded Beth that the room on the cabin was originally intended as a surprise for Janet. It seemed inappropriate now to tell her the purpose of the room, so Beth kept quiet.

"Are you sleeping with her?"

Unsure as to how to answer that question, Beth was slow to respond. After all, Jo *had* made love to Beth, but Beth hadn't actually touched Jo.

Janet folded her arms across her chest. "Well, I guess that answers that." She crossed the floor and began gathering her things. "I'm sorry about being such a bitch with Tracy. I canceled my Los Angeles trip to come and see you. I thought maybe the three of us could go somewhere for a week or so."

Beth cringed. Why now? After all this time, why did Janet wait so long to start trying to make peace with Tracy?

Without thinking about what she was about to do, Beth responded. "Tracy starts to school on Monday."

Janet shrugged. "Fine, you and I can go. Tracy can stay with Ernie and Wanda."

She hasn't changed a bit, Beth realized. "Janet, I'm sorry.

**127**

I don't know what to say." Beth stopped to organize her thoughts. She didn't know how to make this easier. Remembering Ernie's crack about paying the piper, she took a deep breath and plunged in. "Our relationship was about sex. We never talked about make a commitment. There was a time at first when I thought I was in love with you, but now I realize that you came along at a time in my life when I needed to start doing something for myself again."

Beth began pacing. "Tracy was in school and the ranch was as stable as it could ever be."

"So you used me," Janet snapped.

"Don't get holier-than-thou with me," Beth snapped back. "Do you really think I'm stupid enough to believe I'm the only woman you're sleeping with?" Beth was humiliated to admit to herself that until that moment she had never consciously admitted that she suspected she was only one of many women in Janet's little black book.

Janet chuckled. "The little cowgirl does have a bite. I had begun to think you were incapable of anger." Janet tossed her head. "So what does all this mean for us?" she asked.

"I think it would be better if you didn't stop by anymore."

"I see. Ms. Nail Pounder down the hall there moves in and I'm expected to pick up my things and move on. Is that the idea?"

Janet was standing with her arms folded across her chest, and as she grew angrier her arms grew tighter. Beth had a fleeting thought that Janet looked like a boa constrictor coiling around a portion of its own body.

"No one has moved in," Beth countered.

"What about the year we've spent together? Doesn't my being here count for something?"

Beth ran her hand across her forehead and dislodged a streak of mud. She stared at her muddy hands. Her bath water was growing cold. All she wanted to do was scrub herself clean, go to bed, and sleep for hours. On one side she had Janet saying she was ready to make space for Tracy, but she was also more than ready to take off and leave Tracy with Ernie and Wanda. On the other side there was Jo, who one minute was afraid to let Beth touch her but who had only minutes ago suggested that Beth rush back to her room.

Beth was so damn tired. At this very second she didn't care if Janet and Jo both walked out of her life. She was tired of the uproar her life had been in since meeting Janet. Whenever Janet was around tension hung over the house like a heavy fog, and when she wasn't physically around her phone calls trying to arrange ways for them to get away without Tracy invariably came at midnight or later.

And Jo . . . did she want Jo to leave as well? Beth grabbed her head and sighed. She didn't know what she wanted anymore. She wished all of them could just sleep until morning and then sit down and discuss everything rationally without anyone getting hurt. But that wasn't going to happen.

"Janet, in the year we've known each other we've never spent an entire day together."

"That wasn't my fault."

"Hear me out," Beth interrupted. "I don't want to get into a blaming tirade. There's not a single thing in this house that belongs to you, except for what you brought in with you tonight."

"What's that have to do with anything?" Janet demanded.

"We've been seeing each other for a year, and you've never left anything behind." Beth began to pace, knowing she was rambling and not making sense.

"I don't know anything about you other than that you're a trainer for a software company, you own a home somewhere in San Diego, you were born in Montana, and your parents are divorced." Beth was shocked to realize that indeed that was all she knew about the woman she had been having an affair with for a year. Janet walked back to the desk, sat down, and began packing her laptop.

"Janet, you know we never talked about the future. We were two lonely people who came together trying to find some kind of comfort."

The angry look had left Janet's face, and Beth hoped the worse was over.

"Can't we please just enjoy what we had and move on?" Beth asked.

Janet zipped the case holding her laptop. "You're right, Beth." She picked up the case and her bag. "If you're ever passing through San Diego, look me up. We'll go out for a drink or something."

Beth held her breath. She hadn't expected Janet to walk away without more of a scene.

"Oh no," Janet said and turned to Beth. "I just remembered."

"What?" Beth asked wearily.

"The storm. I drove in from Austin tonight, but I have to be in San Antonio tomorrow. I heard on the radio that IH-35 was flooding between here and San Antonio." She shrugged. "It doesn't matter. I'm sure I can find some place to stay if I can't get through."

Beth felt trapped. She didn't want Janet spending the night here, but she couldn't make her leave with the roads being the way they were. Jo was in the guest room.

"You're welcome to use Tracy's room tonight," Beth offered.

"Are you sure?" Janet asked with such hope that Beth was ashamed of not thinking about the weather conditions before. There wasn't even a motel in Dodson.

"Thanks." Janet hesitated at the door. "I'll leave early before anyone gets up."

It was Beth's turn to be thankful.

Janet closed the door softly behind her. Beth trudged to the bathtub. The water was tepid. She released it and refilled the tub. She dumped in a capful of bubble bath. She stripped off her filthy clothes and eased into the hot, soapy water.

Several minutes later, she heard the faint sound of a car motor. That would be either Carl or Ernie leaving, she thought. She decided she would relax in the tub long enough to get her thoughts together and then would go to Jo's room long enough to make sure she was all right. But she would return to her own bed to sleep. Tomorrow she and Jo could talk. She would tell Jo all about Janet and why she had allowed herself to get involved in such a relationship.

Beth wanted to take her time in getting to know Jo. She didn't want to rush this relationship the way she had with Janet. She already knew more about Jo than she did Janet.

Beth had immediately been impressed by Jo's skills as a carpenter. Beth envied the aura of inner strength and confidence that clung to Jo. And Jo's flashes of sadness and vulnerability provoked a strong sense of protectiveness in Beth. While listening to Jo talk about Diane, Beth had heard such devotion that she knew when Jo Merrick loved a woman she loved her totally. Without reservations or conditions.

Beth washed her hair and relaxed for a few minutes. The water began to cool, and she got out and dried off. She grabbed her robe and wrapped it around her. It was time to talk to Jo. As she walked past her bed she noticed the clock at her bedside. It had been over two hours since she had left Jo's room. Jo was probably asleep.

Beth decided she would check to be sure. She walked down the hallway. No light shone beneath Jo's door. Beth tapped lightly. She didn't want to disturb Jo if she was sleeping. There was no response to her knock, so Beth eased the door open. The curtains were open. Enough outside light poured in for Beth to see that the bed had not been turned down. A sense of crushing disappointment settled over her. She checked the bathroom to be sure, but she already knew. Jo was gone.

Going back to her room, Beth glanced toward Tracy's room at the end of the hallway. The door was open. She walked to the doorway, reached in, and flipped on the overhead light. The room was empty. Apparently Janet had decided not to stay. Beth leaned her head against the door frame. Her dad used to tell her to be careful what she wished for. She had wished they would leave her alone, and apparently they both had.


Jo scrubbed herself clean with sure, quick efficiency. She forced her thoughts on getting clean and crawling into bed. After toweling herself dry, she rummaged through the medicine cabinet until she found gauze and tape for a fresh bandage for her leg. There was a large bruise around the cut but no sign of infection.

She pulled on the robe Beth had loaned her. It smelled faintly of roses. She buried her nose in the folds of the robe before pulling away, embarrassed by her need to be close to Beth. She was acting like some lovesick teenager.

She combed her hair. There was no toothbrush, but there was a new tube of toothpaste tucked away in a drawer. She used her finger to brush her teeth as best she could. She was just leaving the bathroom when there was a knock at the door.

She opened the door, expecting to find Beth. Instead she saw a slender woman who would border on classical beauty, except for the hard look in her deep green eyes. Jo suspected that the shade was a result of colored contacts. Black hair, worn short but stylish, framed the stunning face. A sense of smugness emanated from the woman. But there was also an almost tangible sensuality about her. Jo felt frumpy in her tattered, borrowed robe.

She knew without an introduction that this had to be Janet. And Jo could see what had attracted Beth to this woman.

"Sorry to disturb you," Janet began. "Beth was so exhausted, she asked me to let you know we would be leaving early tomorrow morning. We're going to pick up Tracy and go to Dallas for a week or so." She rushed on, not giving Jo an opportunity to speak. Not that Jo would have been able to. She was too shocked by Janet's words and the kick in the gut that Beth hadn't had the decency to tell her this in person.

"I thought it would be best if Beth and Tracy got away for a while and relaxed a little."

Jo wondered about Tracy's schooling. How could she miss the first week or two of school?

"Beth suggested that you send her a bill for whatever amount she still owes you, and she'll mail you a check as soon as we return.

Janet started to leave but stopped. She looked Jo over from head to foot. "You look beat, so we'll try to keep the noise down." She winked at Jo. "It's not often we have time without the little tyke around."

Mortified and angry beyond words, Jo closed the door. She stood rooted to the floor for several minutes. The sound of a car motor finally roused her.

A numbness settled over her as she gathered her dirty clothes and headed to the laundry room. All of her extra clothing was still at the cabin, and the clothing she had been wearing was too filthy to put back on. She couldn't very well go back to San Antonio in a bathrobe.

She methodically planned her return to San Antonio. There would be a bus station or a rental car agency available in Dodson.

She would not let her life fall apart again over Beth Harman's betrayal. If Beth wanted a life with that Barbie doll look-alike, then so be it. Jo had a life to get back to. She refused to acknowledge the pain building inside her.

Jo ached for a cup of coffee but was afraid it would draw them out of their room. Not that they would likely be interested in coffee right now. She couldn't stand the thought of seeing them together. Jo alternated between cussing them and cussing herself for taking so long to make up her mind. Of course Beth wouldn't wait forever. Thirty hours wasn't exactly forever, an angry inner-voice snapped. Was it just yesterday that she had made love to Beth on the riverbank? Just last night that they had lain holding each other as they both pretended to sleep?

There was a large sink in the laundry room, which was nothing more than a small, enclosed section on the back porch. Jo opted to wash out her clothes in the sink rather than to use the washer. She could do it faster. She was grateful that the shirt and shorts were dark and that she didn't have to worry about the stains she knew the dried mud was leaving.

After scrubbing the clothes she threw them into the dryer and went to the back door where she had left her muddy boots. She found a stick and scraped away as much of the mud as she could. The boots were still a mess, but they would do.

Jo sat on the floor leaning against the dryer until she could no longer tolerate the waiting. Snatching the clean but stained and still damp clothes from the dryer, she quickly dressed and went to find some mode of transportation that would get her to Dodson. She didn't care if she had to ride Blossom bareback. She would not spend another minute in this house.

She was surprised and relieved to find Ernie still in the barn rubbing down the horses.

"I need to get home. Can you drive me to the nearest car rental agency or bus station? Or loan me a vehicle I can use for a day or two?" she asked without preamble.

Ernie kept brushing the horse. "You won't find a rental car around here. The closest bus station is Dodson."

"Will you drive me to Dodson? I really need to leave."

Something in her voice made Ernie look at her. After a second he put the brush down. "Let me call home first. Wanda will start to worry if I'm not home soon.

"It'd be better if you waited until the water went down before leaving," he advised, climbing into the driver's side.

"I want to go home." Jo crawled up into the passenger

seat. Against her will her attention was drawn to the house. No lights were on. Everyone was in bed. Probably the same bed, she fumed, tearing her gaze from the mocking darkness only to find Ernie watching her.

"It'd be better if you stayed. You won't ever get anywhere if you keep running away."

Jo's face flamed. She fumbled with the seat belt and fought the tears of frustration that burned her eyes. "I'm not running away. I'm going home." she argued.

With a sigh, Ernie cranked the engine and eased the truck down the graveled lane that led to the main highway. Jo focused her concentration on the dark blurs sliding past her window.

"Thought I heard a car leave earlier," Ernie mentioned.

Jo froze. Beth and Janet had been so anxious to leave together they hadn't even waited until morning. Beth was probably afraid Jo would cause a big scene before they left.

They reached the highway, and the truck increased its speed, putting more and more distance between her and Beth.

Ernie's voice broke the silence. "That's my house up there." He pointed to a house perched high on a hillside. It was only visible by the brightly lit outside security light.

"You must have a great view," she mumbled.

"I don't need to be sitting on a hillside to be able to see the obvious."

"Ernie," Jo snapped, "I appreciate your concern, but I really don't want to discuss this."

She saw him shrug in the green glow of the dash lights. "Jonas Harman, Beth's great-grandfather, gave my grandfather five acres and helped him build that house. It's just me and my wife now, but we raised two beautiful daughters in that house. One of them lives in Seguin with her husband and four kids. The youngest one, Michele, lives in San Antonio with her lover, Angie." His easy reference to his lesbian daughter made Jo turn swiftly to stare at him. Again he shrugged. "It took me a while to see things from her point of view," he admitted. "But she was stubborn and wouldn't give in to my ranting and raving. I told her to give it up and find herself a husband or I'd disown her." He chuckled. "Know what she told me?"

Jo shook her head and smiled at his obvious pride in his daughter.

"She told me to go ahead and disown her. But whether I liked it or not she'd still be my daughter and she'd still be a lesbian." He scratched his chin thoughtfully. "I stewed on that one a few days and finally decided that she was right. That Angie's a good kid. She's going to law school at St. Mary's." He seemed lost in thought for a moment before suddenly launching into his story again.

"My father worked for William, Beth's grandfather, and later for her dad, Bob. When I was growing up I couldn't wait to get away from that house on the hill. I never wanted to see another cow or cactus in my life." He pointed to a bag on the floor. "There's a thermos of coffee in there. Why don't you get us a cup?"

Jo found a plastic cup in the bag, filled it, and passed it to him. "I can drink out of the lid," he said, offering her the cup.

"No. This is fine." She poured coffee into the cup that doubled as the thermos lid and eagerly inhaled its thick rich aroma.

He shrugged and picked up his story. Jo turned her attention back out the window, still somewhat embarrassed that her emotions had been so transparent. Ernie's voice droned on.

"The day I turned eighteen I joined the Army. I had this stupid idea about traveling the world." He sipped his coffee. "The Army didn't waste any time in shipping me to Vietnam. In less than three months, I saw more of the world than I ever want to see again. All I could think of was getting back to that house on the hill. I saved every dollar I could, and when I came back I got a job working for Beth's dad. When my pa died, he left the house to me and my brother. I bought my brother's share of the place."

He fell silent, and Jo waited for the punch line that would sum up the wisdom of his parable. When he continued to quietly sip his coffee, she finally ran out of patience. "And the moral of the story is?"

He glanced at her and shrugged. "I just wanted to tell you about my family."

She stared at him, dumbfounded. When he began to hum quietly to himself she had to laugh. Unconsciously she had been waiting on his story to supply her with a solution for her problems.

"So tell me about the Harman dynasty," she said, relaxing and enjoying the strong coffee that was beginning to make her feel human again.

"Jonas Harman settled here in the late eighteen hundreds. He purchased around two thousand acres. When he died he left everything to William, his only surviving son. William had four boys and two girls. He split up the ranch equally between them when he died.

"Bob, Beth's dad, loved the ranch, and it hurt him to see it broken up. He always dreamed of restoring it to its original size. Two of the kids didn't want the land and sold their shares before he could afford to buy them. Most of the rest of it is still owned by members of the Harman family. Over the years the land that was sold off became divided and subdivided so many times Bob finally had to give up on ever getting it back. He managed to keep his share and one of his sisters sold her share to him.

"During the last few years of his life he started buying a few small pieces of property in town. When he died he left all the town property to Karen and gave the ranch to Beth. I guess he didn't have the heart to split it up again." He drained his cup and handed it back to Jo. She offered to refill it, but he declined. "Karen is married and living in Dallas. Her husband is an investment broker, so they aren't hurting for anything, and besides, she never loved the ranch the way Beth does. The place is in Beth's blood. It almost killed her dad when she left with that good-for-nothing she married." He sighed loudly. "I guess it did kill him."

"Her dad threw her out, didn't he?" Jo asked, unable to keep herself from defending Beth.

"Yeah. It was a bad time for everyone. I tried to talk to him, but he was too damn stubborn, and she's just like him. Once they'd made up their minds neither one of them would listen to reason."

He rubbed his cheek, and Jo heard the raspy scratch of his whiskers against his work-roughened hand. The sound brought back a powerful memory of her own father. After retiring, he and her mom had moved to St. Louis in search of cooler weather and to live near his brother, who had left years earlier for a job at one of the auto plants there.

She missed having them near her. She knew her withdrawal after Diane's death had been confusing for them. Maybe it's time to tell them and clear the air, she thought. As the darkness slid passed her window, the need to talk to her parents grew. She promised herself that she would call them tomorrow and that maybe, in time, she could tell them.

"So you're going to sneak off into the night and let that be that?" Ernie asked, interrupting her thoughts. He cast a sideways glance at her.

"You saw who she left with. What would you have me do? Storm their bedroom and tote her off?" She felt a perverse sense of pleasure when he faltered for a second.

"Did you bother to ask her who she'd rather be with?"

"Ernie! She wasn't exactly hit over the head and dragged away. She walked off with Janet under her own steam. If she hadn't wanted to go, she could've said so."

"Then I guess you'd already told her you didn't want her to go?"

Jo felt the point of the barb slam home. Score one for Ernie, she thought.

His voice softened slightly when he spoke again. "Look. I know it's none of my business, but with her dad gone and all, I feel responsible for her."

"Oh great. Now you're going to become the omnipotent male protector!"

"No, I'm going to be the friend who cares what happens to someone he thinks a hell of a lot of! And I think you'd be a lot better to her and for her than that flit-about Janet."

Their anger left them both shaking, but Jo was warmed by his support of her. She knew he must be as exhausted as she was. She felt bad about dragging him out to drive her all the way to Dodson.

"There's nothing I can do now," she said, letting go of her anger. "Beth made her choice, and it wasn't me."

"You both lost," Ernie retorted, so silently she almost missed it.

"Can we change the subject please?" She turned back to the window to stare into the unknown darkness. They were both exhausted, and the less they said, the better it would be.


Low-water crossings caused them to detour twice. It was daybreak before they reached Dodson.

She listened in disbelief as the station master told Ernie that no southbound buses would be leaving for at least two days due to severe storm damage and a large section of the road being washed out.

"But I have to get to San Antonio," Jo insisted.

"If you can get yourself back around to Interstate 35 you won't have any problems," the station master assured her. "But you can't get there from here." He laughed at his own poor attempt at humor.

Jo turned away from his smoke-stained teeth. "Is there a hotel I can stay at?"

"There's the motel out on the highway, but it's on the other side of the washout."

"What about in town?" Jo asked, exasperated. Would this nightmare never end?

"Nope." With that he turned away and began to methodically stamp a stack of papers on the desk.

"Come on back out to the ranch," Ernie advised.

"No. I'll wait here."

"Jo, be reasonable. You can't sit in this bus station for two days. It could even be longer. They won't know how bad the damage is until the water goes down."

"I'll be fine. I have a credit card if I run out of cash, so I won't go hungry. And I can sleep here on one of these benches." She eyed the hard wooden benches with some trepidation.

Ernie took his hat off and slapped it against his leg. "Blast it. If you won't go back to the ranch, then come and stay with me and my wife. We have plenty of room."

"No, but thanks for the offer."

He eyed her for a minute and started for the door, only to slam back a second later. "Damn, I can't leave you here in this bus station." When she started to speak he held up a finger and stopped her. "Don't you even think about starting that it's-only-because-I'm-a-woman shit. I sure wouldn't want to be stuck sleeping here for two nights, and I sure as hell wouldn't want one of my girls stuck here." He looked around the utilitarian bus station with a glare of distaste.

Jo gazed out the window and found herself staring at a sign for Lone Star Antiques, Reva and Penny's shop.

"If it'll make you feel better, I'll go and stay with some friends here," she said. She turned to find him eyeing her suspiciously.

"Who do you know here?"

"Reva Mifflin, the owner of the antique store just down the street."

He walked to the window to see where she was pointing. "I'll drive you down there," he said at last.

"Ernie, it's less than a block. I can walk that far."

"Well, she might be out of town or something." He put his hat on and headed toward the door.

"You don't believe me!" she exclaimed, following him out the door. "You're going down there to check to make sure I really know her. You think I'm lying."

"I do not."

"Do to." Jo couldn't help but laugh as he stopped to glare at her. After a moment he joined her with a hearty laugh. Jo wiped her eyes. It felt good to laugh.

As they approached the shop, Jo could see the closed sign. "They're not open yet, so why don't I buy you breakfast?" she offered. "It's the least I can do since you drove me all the way here." She took his arm and started toward a flashing café sign.

"I could use something to eat. But I warn you. I have a healthy appetite."

Towering over him, she glanced at his short, wiry frame and laughed to herself. She'd probably eat twice as much as he did.

Jo sat in stunned silence as Ernie cleaned the last of the food off his plate. He had started with a three-egg omelet, an order of ham, hash browns, and biscuits. After polishing that off he'd ordered a large stack of pancakes and six slices of bacon. She'd long since lost track of the amount of coffee he had consumed. He leaned back and sighed contentedly as the waitress removed his plate and filled his cup again.

"I'm sure glad I remembered my credit card," Jo teased, shaking her head in astonishment.

"Just be grateful I hadn't been working all day. I'd have been real hungry then," he returned with a grin.

\* \* \* \* \*

Ernie insisted on waiting for Jo in the truck while she spoke to Reva.

"Everything's all set," she told him after coming out of the shop and poking her head in the window.

"Good," he said, tossing away the toothpick he had been chewing on and starting the truck's engine. "Will I be seeing you back at the ranch any time?"

Jo stepped back and studied her mud-stained tennis shoes. "Probably not."

"What about the room at the cabin?"

Jo shrugged. "I'd be surprised if anything's left to finish," she replied, recalling the swirling water.

"You never know." He continued to sit. "I know she cares for you," he said in an embarrassed tone.

Jo swallowed the lump in her throat. "I thought so too, until last night."

"You don't judge a horse with just one look. You need to know everything about it."

"God!" Jo groaned. "Spare me any more of your analogies."

"Just my opinion," he defended.

She leaned into the truck through the open window. "Ernie, you know what they say. Opinions are like assholes. Everybody has one, and they all stink." She heard his laughter following her as she returned to the shop.

142

# CHAPTER ELEVEN

After shopping at a local department store for a change of clothes, Jo spent the morning playing with Andy while Reva made several calls looking for a particular piece of furniture for one of her regular customers.

"When is Penny supposed to be in?" Jo asked as they sat over a snack of peanut-butter-and-jelly sandwiches. Andy sat on the floor munching and playing with a set of building blocks.

"She should get off around midnight tomorrow night and be here before daybreak. But with the roads so messed up, I'm worried she'll be delayed."

"When is the baby due?" Jo felt a little twinge of uneasiness.

"Not until next week." Reva rubbed her back. "I hope I survive that long," she quipped.

"Just make sure you do," Jo said with a frown. "I know all I want to about childbirth."

"What do you know?" Reva teased, tossing an empty bread bag at her.

"It's messy and hurts like hell."

Reva laughed and absently rubbed the side of her bulging abdomen. She looked around and frowned. "I've got to mop this floor."

"I'll do it," Jo offered.

"Would you mind? The mop really wears me out, but this floor is driving me nuts."

Jo began sweeping the floor with much more vigor than it required. After mopping, she cleaned and stored the mop and bucket in the small bathroom located in the rear of the shop. She found Reva and Andy on the floor dusting the lower shelves and legs of the furniture.

"Can I help?" Jo asked.

"You've already done enough," Reva answered.

Jo looked off through the store windows. If she could stay busy, maybe thoughts of Beth wouldn't haunt her so.

"I'd kind of like to stay busy." She hadn't explained to Reva why she was no longer at the ranch, just that she was trying to get back to San Antonio when the storm hit. She turned back to find Reva watching her.

"There's some more dust rags over there behind the counter. I haven't been able to reach the top shelves in weeks. If you could do those it would help."

As the day wore on, Reva proved to be proficient at keeping Jo busy. She decided the inventory needed to be rearranged according to the time period each piece represented.

Jo strained and grunted as she moved the heavy furniture in accordance to Reva's directions. They were halfway through rearranging the store when Reva changed her mind.

She declared that most of her customers were shopping for a style or particular type of furniture and would have no idea what the time frame was for the piece they needed. Jo's stamina was waning as she struggled to move the items back to their original location.

Jo, working through sheer determination, hadn't slept in more hours than she cared to count. If she could work until she collapsed, she would be able to sleep through the night with no dreams of Diane or Beth.

Even poor Andy wasn't immune from Reva's cleaning frenzy. He had been kept busy picking up his toys from the back of the shop and placing them in the toy box, later sorting a large box of doorknobs.

By the end of the day, Jo was moving on automatic pilot. She and Andy both breathed a deep sigh of relief when Reva finally announced it was time to close the shop. Reva and Penny lived a few blocks from the shop, and the three of them walked.

The house was an old blue-with-white-trim Victorian that at any other time Jo would have spent hours marveling over, but due to her current state of exhaustion, she barely noticed it. Yesterday's trek through the mud and Reva's cleaning fever had left her with the numb relief she was hoping to achieve. She declined Reva's offer of supper and took a quick shower before falling naked across the bed. She was too tired to turn the covers back.

In what felt like only minutes later, someone was shaking her. "Jo, wake up." Jo tried to place the voice. It was familiar, but she couldn't associate it with a face or name.

"Jo. Jo, the baby's coming. I need you to drive me to the hospital in Grayson."

Awareness washed over her. "Grayson! That's almost forty miles away."

"It's the closest hospital. Come on. I've already talked to the doctor, and I've called and left a message for Penny."

Jo jumped up and slipped on her clothes. Her watch told her it was two in the morning. "I'm ready. Come on. Have you got everything?"

Reva sat on the edge of the bed and pressed her hand to her abdomen. "Can you carry Andy to the car? I didn't want to wake him up until I had to."

Fear can be a great motivator, Jo thought as they raced through the streets, her exhaustion forgotten.

"Turn at the next corner," Reva instructed.

"What for?"

"I want to leave Andy with Mr. and Mrs. Scott."

"Can't we just take him with us?" Jo protested. She didn't want to waste any time in getting to the hospital.

"No. I've already called the Scotts to let them know we're coming. Besides, this could take hours and there's no need to put him through it." Reva looked at her and laughed. "Relax. There's plenty of time. It took Penny sixteen hours to deliver Andy."

Glancing back at Andy's nodding head, Jo reluctantly agreed. He would be more comfortable in bed.

Reva guided her to a white frame house. Jo pulled up without turning the motor off. She could see an elderly couple standing in the doorway.

"I'll take him," Jo said, jumping out. "Come on, Andy." She released the seat belt and picked him up.

"Do I got a new sister yet?" he mumbled, rubbing his eye with his fist.

"Not yet, slugger." Jo forced herself not to run. There's plenty of time, she kept telling herself.

Mrs. Scott, a tall, thin woman with overly bright red hair held the door for them. "Just put him on the couch there, sugar, and I'll stay up to watch him."

Mr. Scott thumped over to her. He walked with the support of a cane. "Sure you don't want me to drive?"

Jo noticed his thick glasses and wondered if he could even see to drive. She edged toward the door. "No sir. I'll drive her, but we sure appreciate you and Mrs. Scott watching Andy."

"Oh, glad to do it, sugar." Mrs. Scott patted her arm. "You call us if there's anything else you need."

"Yes ma'am, I will. I'd better go." She raced out the door. With Reva directing Jo back to the main highway, they were soon speeding north toward Grayson.

Jo tried to keep her attention on the road, but Reva's sudden gasps and loud puffing kept distracting her.

"Are you all right?"

"Yes," Reva moaned, "but you'd better hurry up. I don't think I'm going to be as slow as Penny was."

"What do you mean?"

"I believe the baby is about ready to join us."

"Shit! Hold on!" Jo threw on the high beams and pushed the accelerator until the ancient little Volkswagen Golf's speedometer read seventy-five. She was afraid to drive faster, since the car's motor was already knocking. She glanced desperately around them. There wasn't a single light anywhere. "Damn the wide open plains," she muttered.

"How much farther?" Reva groaned only seconds later.

"Not too far," Jo lied. They weren't halfway yet.

"Jo," Reva said, in a voice that was suddenly eerily calm. "I think you'd better pull over."

Relief flooded over Jo. She removed her foot from the accelerator and let the car coast. "A false alarm?" She remembered her mother telling her that she had made three mad dashes to the hospital before Jo was born.

"Not exactly," Reva panted.

"Then what?'

Reva turned to look at her and gave a small apologetic smile. "I think you're about to learn a lot more about childbirth than you ever wanted to know."

Jo slammed on the brakes, took the car out of gear, and stared at her, stunned. There was no way she could deliver a baby. All that blood! Her head spun just thinking about it.

"No! No way. You just wait!" She started to put the car in gear. "I'll have you there in . . ."

Reva's hand was on her arm. "It's too late. She's coming."

Jo sat frozen.

Reva shook Jo's arm. "I'm going to need your help."

"Reva," Jo said in a panic. "I can't." Shame flooded her face. "I faint at the sight of blood."

Reva shook her head and smiled. "You're going to have to help me, and you won't faint."

"I will!" Jo cried.

Reva looked at her closer. "Are you serious?" For the first time Jo saw fear on Reva's face as she grabbed Jo's arm tightly. "Please, tell me you're not serious."

"I'm serious," Jo answered meekly.

"You actually faint at the sight of blood?" She gave her a look of total disbelief.

"Just someone else's," Jo defended, hating the whining sound in her voice.

A contraction hit Reva, and she bit her lip to stifle the groan. She gazed at Jo with eyes full of pain and fear. "I can't do this alone," she said weakly.

Jo felt sweat break out along her collar despite the car's air conditioner. "I don't know what to do."

"Pull the car off the road. We don't want to get rear-ended in case someone should come along."

Dazed, Jo complied.

"I was with Penny when Andy was born," Reva assured her. "I'll help you all I can." Another contraction hit her, causing her to scream out. "Quick," she gasped when she could again speak. "Help me into the backseat."

Jo helped her into the backseat. She braced Reva's back against the side of the car.

"Get me out of these shorts," Reva grunted, trying to pull the shorts down.

Jo did as she was told, her mine racing. Why hadn't she paid more attention to the childbirth stories her mother's friends used to discuss for hours on end?

Reva was rubbing Jo's arm. "It's okay. We can do this. There should be a large bag in the back that has several towels in it. I put them in there for a trip to the coast that we never took. Get them out."

Racing to the back, Jo opened the hatch and found the bag of towels. She skidded to an embarrassed halt by the side of the car. Reva had removed her underwear and reclined naked from the waist down with her legs opened.

"Don't go prude on me now," she said in dismay at seeing Jo's astonished face. "Put a couple of the towels under me." She raised her hips enough to allow Jo to slide the towels beneath her. With the towels in place beneath Reva, Jo spread another one over her nakedness.

"Thank you," Reva sighed after another contraction passed.

Jo suddenly began to recall some of those stories her mother's friends used to discuss. They should have labeled them "the horrors of childbirth: breech births, complications, cesareans, and death." She shook herself. I'm being ridiculous, she scolded. Reva needs me and I can do this.

Thousands of babies are born every day, Jo told herself. Yeah, in hospitals with doctors and drugs, a little voice interjected.

Jo looked around. She needed something to keep her hands busy. "I'm going to make some room." She hopped out and yanked the front seats to their forward-most position and took Reva's small suitcase and stored it in the hatch. When she was finished she crawled into the backseat and knelt on the floorboard by Reva. "How are you doing?" She picked up another towel and wiped the sweat from Reva's face.

Reva's gray eyes met hers. "I think it's time."

Jo's stomach clutched. "What do I need to do?"

"Catch her," Reva said, attempting to smile. "She and I will do the rest."

"What about cutting the cord?" Jo's voice trembled worse than Reva's.

A pain hit Reva. When it subsided she said. "Oh Jesus. I don't know. I hadn't planned on doing this part alone. I've been planning on the doctor taking care of this part."

Jo wiped her forehead against her arm. "Think," she told Reva. "There must be a piece of string or twine in here somewhere." Jo saw Reva's large purse lying between the seats. "How about in your purse? My dad always said my mom toted half a household in her purse. Maybe there's something in there."

"No. I don't think so," Reva paused to breathe. "Wait. Jo, there's some waxed dental floss in my purse. You could break off two pieces and tie them around the cord and then cut between them. Wouldn't that do?"

"It's worth a try." Jo dumped Reva's purse on the floor of the car and dug around until she found the dental floss. "What will I use for scissors?" Jo asked, knowing she was being totally worthless. "Wait. I have a pocket knife. That should work. Shouldn't it?"

"I don't care . . . oh . . . Jo . . . Jo . . . she's coming." Reva gripped the seat. Her scream split the air.

Forgetting her fear and embarrassment, Jo crawled to the edge of the seat. Pushing away the towel that covered Reva, Jo caught her breath at the sight of the top of the baby's head. God, she panicked, how is something this big ever going to come out? There's going to be a lot of blood! Her head began to spin. She backed out of the car onto her knees, pushed her head to the ground, and took several deep breaths. I won't faint, she mentally chanted over and over.

Reva let out another loud scream, and Jo bit her lip. I can't do it. I'll faint and she'll be alone.

"Jo," Reva called. "Jo, where are you?"

"Here," Jo replied weakly. "I'm here."

"Jo, I need you,"

I've got to do this, Jo told herself. She's depending on me. Suddenly Jo recalled the feeling of helplessness she had felt over Diane's pain. There had been nothing she could do to help. But here was a chance for her to do something to help someone she cared about. Taking another deep breath, she crawled back into the car with a new sense of strength. A little more of the baby's head was showing. Another contraction hit Reva, but the head moved no farther.

"Push, Reva."

"I'm trying," she groaned.

The seconds ticked by with nothing happening other than Reva's painful moans. "You're going to have to try harder," Jo insisted.

Reva took a deep breath and strained. The baby's head emerged.

"Look!" Jo shouted. "Look, her head's out."

"Make sure the cord's not around her neck," Reva weakly instructed as she tried to sit up enough to see.

Jo eased the slippery cord around to the back of the baby's neck. Reva pushed a towel toward her. "Clean out her mouth and nose."

Jo used her finger to remove the mucus from the baby's mouth and nose.

"Keep doing that just to be sure," Reva insisted, and Jo realized Reva was worried about her baby.

For a moment their eyes met. "You're both going to be fine. Are you ready to finish this?" Jo asked, unable to keep the smile from her face.

"I think so," Reva said, returning a weak smile. "Don't drop my baby," she warned.

"Not a chance." Jo placed her hand under the baby's head and waited while Reva prepared herself by performing some breathing exercises.

Another contraction gripped Reva, and she screamed.

"Push!" Jo yelled.

"It hurts," Reva cried weakly.

"You have to push!"

Reva bore down, and the shoulders began to slowly push out.

"Harder," Jo cried anxiously.

"I can't. I have to rest." The baby's emergence stopped.

Cradling the baby's head with one hand, Jo used the edge of the towel to wipe sweat from Reva's face.

"It's okay. Rest a minute," she soothed. "Tell me when you're ready to try again."

When Reva nodded a second later, Jo squeezed her hand and once more cradled the baby's head with both hands.

"Give me one more big push. Just one more great big push."

Reva took a shaky breath and bore down. There was a sudden gush and the baby was in Jo's hands. For the moment, nothing in the world existed for Jo except the small slippery bundle in her hands. A new life had just entered the world, and she, Jo Merrick, was the first person to see or touch her.

Jo looked up to see Reva trying to raise up enough to see the baby. Jo placed the tiny still bundle on Reva's stomach. Jo was trying to decide how she could get the baby to respond without that cruel slap on the bottom when the baby gave a tiny kick and a hearty cry.

Reva cried tears of joy, while Jo fumbled with the dental floss to tie off the umbilical cord. It took Jo several seconds to work up the courage to slice through the cord with her pocket knife. When the cord was cut, Jo breathed a sigh of relief and draped a towel over the baby.

"You did a great job," Reva said, and smiled at Jo through her tears. "I was afraid you had fainted on me a couple of times."

"I almost did," Jo admitted through her own tears.

"There's one last thing for you to take care of," Reva said, pointing.

"What?" Jo asked, following the direction Reva indicated. It took Jo a minute to recall enough biology to remember it was the placenta. "What do I do with it?" she asked dumbfounded.

"Just wrap it in one of the towels. The doctor may need to see it."

After carefully wrapping the afterbirth in a towel and setting it on the floorboard, Jo noticed the sucking sounds. Looking up she saw the baby engrossed in her first meal.

Jo continued to stare at the tiny bundle in Reva's arms. I actually did it, she kept repeating to herself. I helped with this incredible event! Jo took a tiny hand into her own and carefully examined the miniature fingers, marveling at their perfection. She glanced up to find Reva watching her.

"If you're ready, I'll get you to the hospital," Jo said, trying to hide her runaway emotions.

Reva took her hand. "Thanks for being here for us. It would have been horrible to be stuck out here with Mr. Scott.

Jo blinked away tears. "I wouldn't have missed it for the world, especially since I didn't disgrace myself by fainting." In a rare display of emotion she kissed Reva's cheek and brushed back her sweat-drenched hair. "Let's get you two in so you'll be ready when Penny arrives."

Dr. Ingram, Reva's doctor, was there to meet them when they arrived at the hospital, and she swept Reva and the baby away on a gurney. Jo was left with an admitting nurse who had a long list of questions, most of which Jo couldn't answer. The nurse finally gave up and told her to wait in the hall. Jo went in the rest room to wash her hands, which were covered with thin streaks of blood. She waited for the familiar dizziness, but it didn't come. Grinning like a fool, she dried her hands and went back into the hallway.

Dr. Ingram stopped by to see her a few minutes later. She

was a tall, sturdy woman with skin the color of warm caramel. She shook Jo's hand.

"Congratulations on doing such a great job on your first delivery."

"Are they okay?"

"Mother and daughter are fine. The baby weighs seven pounds and four ounces, and she's seventeen inches long."

Jo felt an overwhelming sense of pride, as though she personally had something to do with the creation of this perfect child.

"Reva's sleeping now," Dr. Ingram said, while scanning a chart that a passing nurse handed her. "It'll be a while before you can go in." The doctor scribbled on the chart and gave it back to the nurse, who hurried off. Dr. Ingram turned her attention on Jo. "You look like you could use a few hours sleep yourself."

Jo felt as though she was bordering on an emotional overload. She thanked the doctor, muttered excuses about having to park the car, and escaped. She pulled into a slot overlooking a wide-open valley, feeling as weary as the rusty old car looked. She closed her eyes and tried to sort her feelings of exultation, sadness, and exhaustion. So much had happened in such a short time frame. It was overwhelming.

She opened her eyes to see the first rose-tinted rays peeking above the distant line of hills. With the morning sun came her tears, body-racking sobs for losing Diane, for finding and losing Beth, for the indescribable joy of holding a newborn child in her hands, for the privilege of witnessing the glow in Reva's eyes at the first moment of seeing her daughter, and finally for the sheer joy of being alive. When there were no more tears left, Jo rolled all the windows down to catch any stray breeze, pushed and tilted the driver's seat back as far as possible, and slept.

It was after eleven when a hand on her shoulder pulled Jo

back to consciousness. She awoke to find herself being observed by a pair of pale blue-gray eyes.

"Hello." The woman extended her hand. "I'm Penny."

Jo shook off the cotton-cloaked veil of sleep and tried not to stare. This tiny, young woman before her didn't come close to fulfilling the musclebound hulk she had envisioned. It must be hard for this petite, almost delicate creature to hold her own with the rowdy oil field workers, she thought.

Penny smiled with a gentleness that Jo associated with the stereotypical, cookie-baking grandmother.

"Thanks for everything you did for Reva. We weren't expecting the baby until next week or I would have been home sooner."

Jo popped the seat back into position and crawled out of the car, using the time to regain her equilibrium.

"I'm glad I could help," she answered, feeling huge standing next to Penny.

"Reva asked me to find you."

"Is she all right?" Jo asked, suddenly feeling protective. "How's the baby? Did I do something wrong?"

Penny took her hand and squeezed it in a firm and anything-but-delicate grip. "They're both fine, and Dr. Ingram said you did such a great job that you must be a closeted midwife."

Jo laughed, feeling ridiculous at her hovering. "All I did was catch her — and Reva had to tell me to do that."

Laughing, they made their way to Reva's room. She was breast-feeding the baby, and the simple beauty of the act again struck Jo.

"There you are," Reva called. "I was afraid you'd run off."

"She was sound asleep in that hot car."

"Too much excitement for this old body," Jo bantered back.

Penny stepped closer to the bed as Reva pulled the sleeping child from her breast. Penny held the baby while

Reva adjusted her clothing and settled herself back onto the bed.

"We've just gotten off the phone with Andy. After a family conference, we wanted to formally introduce you to Kerri Jo Mifflin-Wayne," Penny said.

"We thought she should carry the names of the first three women in her life, and Merrick-Mifflin-Wayne seemed a lot for her to have to learn to spell," Penny said with a contagious grin.

"I don't know what to say," Jo answered, both amazed and honored.

"Say it's okay with you so we don't have to redo all that paperwork," Penny begged.

"I think I'll remember the paperwork longer than the birth pains," Reva agreed.

Jo was unable to stop the silly grin from sliding onto her face. "Of course it's all right. I'm honored you would even consider it, but shouldn't it be someone closer, a grandmother or something?"

"Don't you realize that if you hadn't been there and Mr. Scott had delivered her, we'd have had to name her Kerri Elmer?" Reva shook her head in mock horror.

"Well, do me a favor," Jo began. "If you decide to have any more children, I'd prefer to build the crib the next time." They all burst into laughter. Their merriment was interrupted by a nurse who came in to announce that Dr. Ingram had released Reva and that she and Kerri could go home.

Shocked, Jo followed the retreating nurse. "Isn't it too soon?" she demanded. "I thought she'd have to stay for a day or two."

The nurse looked at her and shook her head. "The birth was normal. Well, as normal as a birth in a backseat can be." When Jo still wasn't convinced, the nurse patted her arm. "Honey, they're both fine and will rest much better at home."

Reva, Kerri, and Penny rode back in Penny's Jeep Cherokee. Jo drove back alone in the battered Golf. She had developed a soft spot for the odd-looking heap that had given its best when needed. She took her time in going back and enjoyed seeing the tiny shoots of green the rain had caused to sprout.

The floodwater was already receding from everywhere except the lowest areas, leaving behind patches of mud and a fresh burst of vegetation.

During the next few days the brown sun-baked landscape would be transformed into fields of green that would soon again be dried and baked without more rain. It was an endless cycle that was as dependable as the sunrise. A sense of peacefulness settled over Jo that she hadn't known since Diane's diagnosis. She took a deep breath of the hot, humid Texas air and slowly exhaled. It was time for her to go home and put her life back together. If the bus wasn't running yet, she would walk or do whatever it took to get there.

# CHAPTER TWELVE

Jo called the bus station when she returned to Dodson. The roads were passable, and a bus to San Antonio was leaving in three hours.

Penny, Reva, and the kids arrived just as Jo was dropping off Reva's car. At first, Andy pleaded with Jo to stay with them, but she was soon forgotten in his excitement over his new sister. Penny walked the few blocks to the station with Jo.

"I don't even know you," Penny began, "but I'll always be grateful for everything you did."

"I'm glad I was able to help." Impulsively Jo leaned down to hug Penny. "You have a wonderful family."

"Will you come back to visit?"

Jo looked away. "I'd like that. I've got a lot of things to take care of, but I'd like to come back soon."

"You're welcome any time."

It was midafternoon when Jo entered her hot, musty-smelling home. She opened all the windows and collapsed onto the bed. The excitement and stress of the prior few days were soon lost in the release of sleep.

The phone rang early that following morning, but Jo ignored it. Elsie was still in Vermont with her sister, and Beth was with Janet. After several rings the caller gave up and Jo was again grateful she hadn't given in to Elsie's badgering to get an answering machine.

The house was hot and humid even with the windows open. Jo stretched and thought about Diane. The usual pain felt softer. Thinking about Beth was in some ways more painful, so she pushed those thoughts away. She had spent the last two years hurting, and now it was time to get her life in order. She would sort out her feeling for Beth later, but right now she needed to do things for herself. She swung her feet off the bed. She had a dozen things to take care of, starting with calling her parents. Her mom answered the phone on the second ring.

"Hi, Mom."

"Jo! Honey is that you?"

Jo heard her father in the background.

"How are you?" her mom asked.

Jo hesitated before answering, knowing her dad would be picking up the extension before she could reply.

"How are you, JoJo?" his voice boomed. She smiled at the nickname. She would never let anyone other than her father call her JoJo.

"I'm good, Dad. How are you two doing?" She sat back in her chair, preparing for the ten-minute spiel she'd receive as they both gave her a rundown on what they had been doing since she had last talked to them. A twinge of nervousness ran through her as she again thought about coming out to them.

Her parents were pretty liberal people, but she couldn't remember them ever discussing homosexuality. What if they don't know what it means and I have to explain it? She was so wrapped up in her thoughts that she almost missed her dad asking about what she had been working on recently. She launched into the story of building the room onto Beth's cabin. Her dad asked a dozen questions on the construction, during which time she could hear her mom rattling dishes in the kitchen. All the while they were talking, she was mentally preparing herself to tell them.

"How's Uncle Roger?" she asked to delay the process. Her parents launched into a new narrative on every family member. After nearly an hour her father made his usual statement about running up her phone bill. It's now or never, she agonized. Taking a deep breath she blurted. "Mom, Dad, I need to tell you something." Probably for the first time in her life both of her parents were silent at the same time. She cleared her throat. "It's something I've wanted to talk to you about for some time now, but I've been putting it off. I don't want to hurt either of you, but during the last couple of years there's been so many things I couldn't tell you. I wish I'd had the courage to tell you sooner, because I know now that I needed you. I'm not blaming you," she added quickly before rushing on. "I think you both would have understood and supported me thorough everything. It was me. I just wasn't ready to reach out." Jo knew she was rambling and probably had them totally confused by now. It was time to say the words. Her throat felt tight. Diane, she whispered to herself, this is for you. I know I'm late in doing this, please forgive me.

"Mom, Dad, I'm gay."

"Oh, thank God," her mother sighed. "I thought you were ill." Jo's ears roared from the overabundance of blood her pounding heart was sending out. She misunderstood me, Jo groaned. She waited for her dad to say something. When he didn't she prodded him. "Dad?"

He exhaled. "I'm here, JoJo."

"Well, say something," she pleaded.

"What's to say?" her mother asked. "It's not like we're surprised, honey."

"You're not?" Jo asked, unable to believe what she was hearing.

"Christ, JoJo. We may be old, but we're not senile. We've known since you were in high school."

"Why didn't you say something?"

"We didn't want to pry," they both sputtered at once.

"What if we'd been wrong?" her mother reasoned.

"Or you didn't know yet?" her father added. "We knew you'd tell us when you were ready."

Jo ran a hand over her face. She wasn't sure what to say or think. "At first I didn't think it was important. It seemed too private to talk about. And then when it came time to tell, you I couldn't. I was afraid you'd be disappointed in me," she said, her voice shaking.

Her mother sighed. "Honey, I'll be honest. It's not the life we'd have chosen for you. We both were sort of hoping for grandchildren, but we love you. If you're happy, it's enough for us."

Still wanting to hear what her father had to say Jo took another deep breath. "Dad?"

"Your mother's right. We didn't ask anyone how to live our lives, and it wouldn't be right for us to try and tell you how to live yours. As though you ever did anything you didn't want to do anyway," he added with mock gruffness.

Her mom cut in. "We tried to reach out to you when Diane died, but you were hurting so much you pushed us away."

Jo heard the pain in her mother's voice and was sorry for having caused it. "I'm sorry, Mom."

"Honey, don't apologize. We all handle things at our own pace. Your dad and I were probably wrong not to say something to you sooner, but you've always been such a private person. Even as a child you kept everything inside. When

Diane become ill we didn't want to intrude or make things harder for you."

Jo wiped tears from her eyes as her mom continued.

"We would have done anything we could to have prevented you from going through that. We tried so hard to get you to let us come out and stay with you for a while."

Jo remembered the calls her mom had made suggesting they come out and stay with her a while and how she had held them off.

"Your mom wanted to fly out and be with you, but I talked her out of it. I thought it would make things hard on you. Maybe I was wrong," her dad admitted.

Jo couldn't wipe the tears away fast enough. They streamed down her cheeks. "No, Dad. I wouldn't have been comfortable trying to tell you then." Jo could hear her mom sniffle. "I've always felt so bad that I broke my promise to Diane," her mother said.

"What promise?" Jo asked. As far as she knew Diane and her parents had barely spoken to each other. The only time they had met was when her parents had surprised her.

"Now may not be a good time to bring that up, Maureen," her father cautioned.

"What are you talking about?" It was Jo's turn to be confused.

"Diane called us about a week before she died. We talked for a long time. She didn't want you to have to face her death alone, and she knew you wouldn't ask for help. She loved you so much, Jo. I promised her we would do all we could, but I'm afraid we didn't do enough."

Jo didn't know what to say. Diane had never mentioned talking to Jo's parents. "You did all I would allow," she admitted. "I think Diane knew that ultimately it was up to me to reach out." Suddenly Jo began to talk. She told her parents about how hard the two years after Diane's death had been. She told them about Penny and Reva and how she had delivered their daughter.

"I knew you were destined to be a doctor," her mother interjected.

And finally she told them about Beth and Tracy. After hearing her out, her father offered his advice.

"If you love her, don't give up on her," he said.

"Call her," Jo's mother urged. "You've got to tell her how you feel."

Jo promised to think about their suggestions.

An hour later, they ended the call with Jo promising to call more often and her parents promising to pry more.

Jo felt as if a huge weight had been lifted from her shoulders. There was a lot for her to do. She started by notifying the insurance company about her truck and tools.

She picked up an insurance-provided rental car to use before withdrawing enough money from the savings account funded by Diane's life insurance money to have a new air-conditioning unit installed in the house.

After returning home, she changed into a pair of cutoffs and tank top and began ripping up the threadbare carpet in the living room. There was a hardwood floor beneath, and she set about restoring it.

Two days later Jo called the insurance company and learned that her truck had been written off as a total loss. They informed her she would be receiving a check for the truck and its contents soon. When they quoted her the amount of the settlement, she was satisfied. It would be enough to replace the vehicle and most of the tools.

She added finding another truck to her list of things to do. She scanned the newspaper daily for possibilities. Three days later she found a great deal on a used Ford pickup that was being sold by a guy in the military who had received unexpected orders and was being shipped to Korea. She decided to wait until later to replace the tools. Most of them she could do without for a while.

* * * * *

The phone rang several times during the next two weeks, but Jo ignored it. She wanted no outside distractions. She needed to be completely focused on herself and her house. Each day she felt her spirit grow stronger. Her soul was healing.

She had received a postcard from Elsie complaining she hadn't been able to reach Jo by phone. She had wanted to let Jo know that she had decided to stay a few extra days with her sister who was feeling better.

When the flooring was completed, Jo repainted the small house inside and out. She pulled weeds, planted grass and flowers, and got the yard in shape. She worked from early morning until exhaustion forced her to stop. She was hanging new curtains in the living room when there was a loud pounding on her door late one afternoon. Jo's aching muscles caused her to groan as she climbed down from the chair to answer it.

"Where in the hell have you been?" Elsie demanded, nearly knocking Jo down when she charged through the door.

"Right here," Jo answered, attempting to give Elsie a quick hug. But Elsie was in too big a huff to stand still. "I got home this afternoon and had a half-dozen messages from Beth Harman. She said she's been trying to reach you for over a week. I called you myself less than twenty minutes ago."

Jo remembered the phone ringing and shrugged, trying to curb her excitement that Beth had been trying to contact her. "What did she want?" she asked, attempting to sound nonchalant.

Elsie's steam ran out as quickly as it had built. She was now lost in observing the freshly painted walls, new curtains, and flooring. "My god, you've finally fixed it up," she whispered. "The air conditioner is even working!"

"Let's hope it is. For what I paid it should run the rest of my life."

"What happened? What finally made you decide to fix it?

164

Is that your truck in the driveway?" she demanded without waiting for answers.

"I decided it was time to fix the place up, and yes, that is my truck in the driveway." Jo knew Elsie was going to want details and, strangely enough, she didn't mind telling her. It was time to let the people she loved into her life. "Why don't you give me time to get cleaned up and I'll take you to dinner? My treat."

"What?" Elsie stared at her in amazement. "Did you rob a bank or win the lottery while I was gone?"

Jo brushed her hands through her hair. "No. I just decided to use some of the money I already had." Jo watched the dismay sweep across Elsie's face. "Are you hungry?" Jo persisted.

Elsie nodded, seemingly unable to speak.

"Good. Give me time for a quick shower." Jo started toward the bathroom.

"Jo, you have to call Beth Harman first. She's really upset that she hasn't been able to get in contact with you. Frankly, I was ready to call the police. You never disappear like that. Where were you?" Elsie was watching her closely.

"It's a long story. I'll tell you over dinner," she promised, trying not to show her personal turmoil over the mention of Beth's name. "Did she say what she needed?"

"She wants to talk to you about the room you were building for her."

Jo blinked a couple of times. The cabin had completely been erased from her thoughts. She had kept herself so busy during the past two weeks that there had been no time for thoughts of anything else. The carpenter in her began to wonder how much damage the river had caused.

She realized Elsie was still watching her. She didn't want to talk to Beth with Elsie standing there listening. It would be hard enough without an audience. She nodded and turned back toward the bathroom.

"I'll call her tomorrow morning."

Elsie wasn't going to be put off so easily. "Jo, what's wrong? This isn't like you. Look at yourself. You must've lost ten pounds while I was gone. You bought a new truck and you've completely redone this house. Now what's going on?"

Jo laughed as Elsie assumed her seriously pissed drill-sergeant stance. Experience told Jo that nothing short of the full story would suffice. "Can we compromise here? You call for a pizza while I shower. I'll tell you everything that's happened since we last spoke, then you go home and I'll call Beth."

Elsie stood firm for a moment before gradually relenting.

Jo took her time in the shower. It would be hard to put everything that had happened in the last few days into words. She was pulling on a clean shirt when Elsie pounded on the door to tell her the pizza had arrived.

"Hurry up," Elsie ordered. "You've hidden long enough. You know I can't tolerate cold pizza."

"Elsie," Jo began as she stepped out of the bathroom, tucking her shirt into her shorts. "You are probably the only person on earth who doesn't like cold pizza."

Elsie shudder. "It's disgusting, so let's eat."

Elsie began a running dialogue about Vermont and the beautiful countryside. Jo knew she would not press her for details until after they had eaten, so she took advantage of Elsie's strange quirk and ate slowly. When she was stuffed and unable to avoid the inevitable, Jo pushed away from the table and began to clear away the mess.

Elsie placed a hand on her arm. "No more stalling. What's going on?"

Jo took a deep breath and sat down. "I'm not sure I really understand it myself," she began. "I fell in love with Beth Harman, nearly died in a flood, delivered a baby, and discovered the simple beauty of life all over again."

Elsie stared at her. "Jo, I was only gone a couple of weeks. Back up and start at the beginning. And if you love Beth, why are you avoiding her? Why is she calling me looking for you?"

"I thought she loved me, but there was someone else in the picture."

Elsie sat back and sighed. "The beginning, Jo. Start at the beginning."

Jo began to fill her in on what had been happening to her.

It was after eleven-thirty before Elsie left with a promise to drop by the next day to check on her. Due to the late hour, Jo was granted a brief reprieve. She wouldn't have to call Beth until tomorrow morning. Feeling both physically and emotionally drained from all the redecorating and soul searching she had been doing, Jo dropped into bed. The one thing that Jo hadn't told Elsie was that she was certain she knew why Beth was trying to contact her. She was calling to settle payment for the work Jo had done on the room. Janet had told Jo that she should send Beth an invoice and that Beth would mail Jo a check, but Jo hadn't bothered. So she was sure Beth was trying to settle her financial obligations.

Someone knocking on the front door pulled Jo from a deep sleep. For a moment she stretched her naked body and enjoyed the cool luxury and privacy the new air conditioner and curtains provided. She knew it was Elsie at the door, so she took her time in pulling her robe around her and tramping to the door. At a fresh series of pounding, Jo called out.

"Hold on to your britches, I'm coming." She unlatched the chain and pulled the door open. "For crissake, Elsie, couldn't you —" She stopped and gaped stupidly at Beth Harman. For a long second they stood staring at each other. Jo recovered first. "Sorry, I thought you were Elsie."

"You shouldn't open your door without checking to see who's there first."

"Did you drive all the way to San Antonio to impart those pearls of wisdom?" Jo asked, glad to see Beth despite herself.

"No, I had to drive in because you won't extend the common courtesy of answering your phone," Beth countered, obviously upset.

"It's my damn phone. I'll answer it when and if I want to!" Jo snapped back.

"Well," Beth sputtered before running out of steam. A small smile broke through, and she slipped her hands into her pockets. The simple act took the starch out of Jo's sails, and she smiled in return.

"Maybe you should close the door and we could start over," Beth said.

"Why don't you come in and sit down while I make some coffee?" They went inside to the kitchen. Jo put the coffee on and turned to find Beth watching her. She realized she was wearing nothing but her robe and pulled it closer to her. "The coffee will be ready in a minute. If you'll excuse me, I'll get dressed."

Beth sat at the kitchen table and willed her heart to slow down. She forced her breathing to drop to a normal level. The house smelled of new paint and fresh varnish. She hadn't thought it would be so difficult to be near Jo again, but she had been wrong. Why had she come on like such a tyrant? Why was it that every time she got around this woman she ended up feeling like her entire nervous system had been dumped in a blender and pureed? She should never have listened to Ernie's wild idea. It had been his suggestion that Beth drive in to San Antonio and contact Jo. Of course, she admitted, he didn't have to talk too hard to convince me. Now it seemed silly to have come barging in unannounced. She could have mailed the insurance papers to Jo and asked her to fill them out. Or you could have done it yourself, her conscience nagged.

Her insurance company needed a comprehensive list of the

tools Jo had lost at the cabin during the flood before they would send a settlement check to Jo. Beth knew she could have probably remembered everything or simply have ridden over to the cabin and dug through the mud, but she convinced herself without much effort that she should contact Jo for a complete listing. Any excuse to hear her voice, her conscience nagged again.

Beth debated with herself for the next several days as to why Jo had left without telling her and whether she should call. She finally came to the conclusion that Jo still wasn't ready.

She tried to stay active, but for once there didn't seem to be enough to do on the ranch to keep her busy. The house took on a tomblike atmosphere with Tracy in school.

After a few days of her sharp tongue, Ernie began to suggest that Beth needed to call Jo and work things out. She smiled to herself at his less-than-subtle hinting that she was being a bitch. And then Tracy started her campaign to bring Jo back.

For two days, Tracy would report every little item that might possibly need repairing to Beth. First the barn needed painting, then the corral needed a new post, and a water faucet was dripping. On and on the list went until Beth caught Tracy with a hammer prying a board loose from the barn.

"What are you doing?" Beth demanded when she rounded the corner of the barn and caught Tracy in the middle of her act of sabotage.

Tracy quickly turned the hammer around and began to pound the board back down. "The barn needs fixing," Tracy informed her. "You should call Jo."

Beth felt her anger fade. She knew Tracy had gotten attached to Jo. "Sweetie, Jo had to go back home. She has other work she needed to do."

"Like what? She ain't finished my room yet."

"Hasn't finished," Beth corrected.

169

"Ain't!" Tracy screamed, stomping her foot and throwing the hammer down. She turned and started away.

"Tracy Harman. You get back here this minute."

Tracy stopped and slowly turned around. Her eyes filled with tears. "Why can't Jo come back?"

"Come here," Beth knelt down and pulled Tracy into her arms. "Honey, I know you miss Jo, but she had to go home."

"Why?" Tracy demanded. "Doesn't she like us no more?"

"Of course she likes you, sweetie, but she has to work."

"Can't she work here?"

"No. There's not enough work, and besides, I don't have enough money to pay her to fix everything that needs fixing."

"Couldn't she just live here like Janet did sometimes?"

Beth hesitated, not sure what to say next.

"Don't you like Jo no more?" Tracy asked, staring into Beth's eyes.

"Yes," Beth admitted. "I like Jo a whole lot."

"Then tell her to come back. She'll listen to you."

The letter from the insurance company asking for a complete list of everything that had been damaged at the cabin arrived in that day's mail. Beth decided it was an omen and began her one-person telephone campaign directed toward finding Jo Merrick.

This time when Ernie stepped in he wasn't quite so subtle. He boldly told Beth that any woman worth having was certainly worth going after. An hour later she had left Tracy with Wanda and headed to San Antonio.

Now here she sat with a pocket full of papers and her tongue sticking to the roof of her mouth from fear. What could she say that wouldn't send Jo running again? She had already told her she'd wait as long as necessary.

Jo came out of the bedroom dressed in shorts and a tank top. Beth tried not to stare at the muscles in Jo's thighs that rippled sensuously when she walked.

"Would you like some coffee?" Jo asked, taking down two cups when Beth nodded.

She filled the cups and, without asking, added the single spoon of sugar that Beth always took. The simple act shredded Beth's resolve. Jo was setting the cups down, but Beth couldn't see through the tears burning her eyes. She jumped up from the table. She had to get out before she made a complete fool of herself. Her hand was on the doorknob when Jo's reached around her and held the door shut.

"I think it's time we both stop running." The words were whispered in Beth's ear and opened the gates that had been holding back the tide of emotions building within her. Beth turned and looked up into the smoldering eyes that had been haunting her.

"I know there's Janet, but —"

Beth interrupted her. "I told you before, Janet was a mistake that I don't want to talk about right now. Just know that Janet is out of my life for good."

"I want you so bad I ache," Jo said in a hoarse whisper.

Beth continued staring at her. "I can't do this unless you're ready to let me make love to you also," she answered, holding her breath, waiting for an answer. Would she be able to walk away if Jo said no?

A small smile tugged at Jo's lips. "Would you believe me if I tell you I may die if you don't touch me?" Without waiting for an answer her lips brushed across Beth's cheek and inched their way along her neck.

"Where's the bedroom?" Beth demanded, running her hands through Jo's unruly hair. Jo led the way and pulled Beth down onto the bed she had just vacated minutes earlier. She pulled Beth beneath her and again began her leisurely journey along her neck.

"Not this time," Beth insisted, rolling Jo over and pinning her to the bed. She stripped Jo's clothes away with two quick movements before standing and shedding her own clothes. She could see the want in Jo's eyes, but she had waited too long for this moment to rush. Straddling Jo's hips she lowered her body and ran her tongue along Jo's rib cage. She nibbled her way across the tops of Jo's breasts, careful not to touch the rock-hard nipples. Jo tried to arch them toward Beth's warm mouth, but Beth dodged the move and continued her sensual journey. Her lips and tongue sampled the silky smoothness of Jo's throat before her tongue made a complete exploration of the curves and textures of her ears.

Jo grasped Beth's hips and was rocking against them by the time Beth finally relented and wrapped her lips around the rosy nipple. She almost lost control herself when she slipped her hand between their bodies and made a teasing pass over Jo's wetness.

Without warning Jo's arms wrapped around her and with relative ease turned her over onto her back. Beth was about to protest when Jo's hand clamped strongly around Beth's and pressed it deeper into her. A low groan started somewhere far inside Jo and swiftly escalated to the savage guttural sounds of sexual release. Beth found herself pushing desperately against the tangle of hands that was jammed between them. The bed creaked wildly until at last the dam broke and for those few brief moments they were joined together in the ultimate embrace.

# EPILOGUE

Beth slid the last hamburger patty onto the already laden platter that Jo held. "Take those on in while I gather everything up," Beth said, pulling her coat tighter around her.

"I love you," Jo said with a smile, amused at Beth's valiant attempt to give Tracy everything she wanted for her seventh birthday. Tracy had not quite grasped the concept that barbecuing was not a January event. When she had insisted she wanted barbecued burgers for her birthday, Beth had relented. The temperature had dropped into the low twenties during the night and hadn't improved much during the day.

Beth, nose red with cold, smiled and kissed Jo. "You hold on to that thought," she instructed. "Now get inside before the food freezes."

Jo wasted no time in returning to the warmth of the kitchen. Reva held the door open for her.

"Does Beth need any help?" she asked, shutting the door against the cold.

"No. She'll be here in a minute." Jo set the platter down and shrugged out of her coat. From the living room she heard Andy squeal.

"Sounds like someone's having fun," Beth said, pushing through the door.

"Penny and the kids are playing with the puppy," Reva explained, taking the pan and things Beth was holding.

"The puppy." Beth moaned and threw Jo another I-can't-believe-you-actually-did-that look.

"We'll keep it outside," Jo promised.

"Yeah, sure you will," Beth said, rolling her eyes. "It's too cold, Mom," she mimicked Tracy's pleading voice. "You know it'll be used to living in the house by spring and I'll never get it out."

"It's only a puppy," Jo reasoned, unwrapping buns and placing them on a large cookie sheet to heat. Reva wisely scurried out of the kitchen.

"It's a Saint Bernard," Beth cried, exasperated. "I can't believe you bought her a Saint Bernard for her birthday."

"She saw it in the pet store and fell in love with it," Jo defended. "What was I supposed to do?" She slid the buns into the oven.

"Learn to say no," Beth explained. Unable to be angry, a smile played along her lips as she walked to Jo and slid her arms around her. "You can't give her everything she wants."

"Why not?" Jo asked, pulling her closer and running her hands over her hips. "You give me everything I want."

"Don't start something you can't finish," Beth warned, but raised her lips to Jo's. The sound of approaching voices from down the hallway broke them apart.

"I'm hungry," Tracy declared, running and wrapping her arms around Jo's legs as the rambunctious puppy raced beneath the table barking. "Ginger rolled over," Tracy informed them in a voice filled with pride as she bent to scoop up the bundle of fur.

"I believe *fell* over is a better description," Penny corrected, handing Kerri to Reva, who sat down at the table.

"Kerri can roll over," Andy declared, not wanting to be outdone. They all laughed, and Jo swung Andy into her arms, hugging him tight. "And Kerri is much quieter, isn't she?"

"Not when she cries," he said, shaking his curly head.

"Yeah. She gets real loud," Tracy agreed, pushing her hair away from her eyes.

Jo knelt down and pulled Tracy to her, hugging the two kids and puppy tightly before setting Andy down. Standing, she reached for Kerri.

"Tracy, get Ginger out of the kitchen," Beth insisted. "then go wash your hands. We're almost ready to eat."

"Come on, Andy. Let's get you cleaned up some too," Reva said, taking his hand.

"Guess I'd better go too," Penny said, following the group out.

Jo rocked Kerri on her lap. "Have you ever thought about having another baby?" she asked.

Beth turned to stare at her. "I've never given it much thought. Why?"

"I just wondered."

Beth walked to the table and placed her hand on Jo's shoulder. "Do you want to have a baby?"

"Me?" Jo shrieked.

"I already have one," Beth reminded her with a slight smile.

Jo remained silent for a while. "I guess one's enough," she replied, tossing Beth a sheepish grin.

"I think so too," Beth agreed. "I love Tracy, but I'm looking forward to the day when I can attack you anywhere and anytime I want to without having to worry about getting caught." As if to reinforce her point, Tracy came bounding in.

After dinner, Tracy and Andy disappeared to Tracy's room to play with her new toys and Ginger. Jo lay on the floor dangling a small mobile of butterflies above Kerri. Beth was in a chair with her sock-clad feet resting against Jo's thighs. Reva and Penny sat on the couch with Reva's head on Penny's shoulder.

"Jo, how are you adjusting to country living?" Penny asked, referring to Jo's recent move to the ranch.

"It's great," Jo replied, throwing Beth a smoldering glance.

"Are you having trouble finding work?" Reva asked.

"Tell them," Beth prompted, shaking Jo with her foot.

"What?" Reva sat up, sensing a secret.

"I made a china cabinet and a hutch. You know, just curious to see if there was a market for them."

"And?" Reva prompted.

"I gave photos to Elsie Brown, a friend of mine, and she showed them around. A woman from Austin called yesterday. She sells specialty furniture. She wants to buy them and said she'd be interested in seeing anything else I make."

"We're going to convert the south end of the barn into a workshop," Beth burst out, unable to stay silent any longer.

"Will you still do construction?" Penny asked.

"I'll probably do a few small jobs until I see if this furniture venture is going to take off," Jo replied. "And we're going to rebuild the room in the cabin. The flood did a lot of damage, but for now my main focus will be on building furniture. It feels right."

They talked about Jo's new venture for several minutes. When the discussion settled down, Penny turned to a more serious topic. "Have you talked to Tracy about her father yet?"

Jo picked up Kerri and balanced her on her thighs before settling back against Beth's leg. Jo and Beth had decided to confide in Reva and Penny about Tracy's father and get their opinion on how to tell her or if she should be told. They all agreed it would be best for Tracy to hear it from Beth first, and that Beth should wait and see how Tracy handled the initial information before deciding how much to tell her. When it came time for the discussion, Jo and Beth both sat down to tell Tracy.

"Yeah," Beth sighed. "I'm not sure how much she understood. She had a lot of questions about her father, and I didn't know whether to tell her everything now or just give it to her piecemeal. Jo thought it was better for her to learn everything at once."

"I was afraid she'd always think we were holding something back if we just gave it to her in bits and pieces," Jo explained, hoping her decision was right.

"Kids understand a lot more than we think," Penny reasoned.

"You were probably right to tell her everything," Reva agreed.

"Her questions about us were a lot harder," Jo said with a sigh. "I'm not sure what we would have done without the advice you two gave us."

"I guess coming out is never easy," Beth said, stroking Jo's hair. "No matter who you're telling."

"Speaking of coming out," Jo said and grinned. "My parents want to come visit next summer."

"Oh, meeting the in-laws." Reva grimaced and clutched her face.

Jo had learned that neither Penny nor Reva's parents would accept their lifestyle and had withdrawn from their lives.

"They sounded pretty excited when I spoke to them on the phone," Beth said. "I'm looking forward to meeting them."

"They love her already," Jo replied and rolled her eyes. "She gave them a granddaughter."

"You can too, sweetheart," Beth teased.

The kids and Ginger came tearing in and saved Jo from replying. Tracy settled beside Jo, and Andy crawled between Penny and Reva.

Jo felt a sense of happiness and completeness settle over her as she gazed around at her new family. Beth's hand slipped to her shoulder, and Jo reached up to squeeze it. As the cold January wind whipped sharply around the house, Jo snuggled back deeper between Beth's legs. The warmth of the love within that room would keep her warm forever.

## About the Author

Frankie J. Jones is the author of *Rhythm Tide, Whispers in the Wind,* and *Captive Heart.* She enjoys travel, long walks, and lazy Sundays.

Publications from
# BELLA BOOKS, INC.
*The best in contemporary lesbian fiction*

P.O. Box 201007    Ferndale, MI 48220
Phone: 800-729-4992
Web:www.bellabooks.com

ROOM FOR LOVE by Frankie J. Jones. 192 pp. Jo and Beth must
overcome the past in order to have a future together.
ISBN 0-9677753-9-6    $11.95

THE QUESTION OF SABOTAGE by Bonnie J. Morris. 144 pp. A
charming, sexy tale of romance, intrigue, and coming of age.
ISBN 0-9677753-8-8    $11.95

SLEIGHT OF HAND by Karin Kallmaker writing as Laura Adams.
256 pp. A journey of passion, heartbreak and triumph that reunites
two women for a final chance at their destiny.  ISBN 0-9677753-7-X    $11.95

MOVING TARGETS: A Helen Black Mystery by Pat Welch.
240 pp. Helen must decide if getting to the bottom of a mystery
is worth hitting bottom.                ISBN 0-9677753-6-1    $11.95

CALM BEFORE THE STORM by Peggy J. Herring. 208 pp. Colonel
Robicheaux retires from the military and comes out of the closet.
ISBN 0-9677753-1-0    $11.95

OFF SEASON by Jackie Calhoun. 208 pp. Pam threatens Jenny
and Rita's fledgling relationship.        ISBN 0-9677753-0-2    $11.95

WHEN EVIL CHANGES FACE: A Motor City Thriller by Therese
Szymanski. 240 pp. Brett Higgins is back in another heart-pounding
thriller.                            ISBN 0-9677753-3-7    $11.95

BOLD COAST LOVE by Diana Tremain Braund. 208 pp. Jackie
Claymont fights for her reputation and the right to love the woman
she chooses.                         ISBN 0-9677753-2-9    $11.95

THE WILD ONE by Lyn Denison. 176 pp. Rachel never expected
that Quinn's wild yearnings would change her life forever.
ISBN 0-9677753-4-5    $11.95

SWEET FIRE by Saxon Bennett. 224 pp. Welcome to Heroy — the
town with the most lesbians per capita than any other place on the
planet!                              ISBN 0-9677753-5-3    $11.95

# Visit
# Bella Books
## at

# www.bellabooks.com